Prelude to Death in D Minor

Michel Marchaud

BearManor Media
1317 Edgewater Drive #110
Orlando, Florida 32804
www.bearmanormedia.com

Hardcover: ISBN 978-1-62933-594-0
Paperback: ISBN 978-1-62933-593-3

Printed in the United States of America.
Book design by Brian Pearce | Red Jacket Press.

Dedication

Frederic Francois Chopin
March 1, 1810 to October 17, 1849

"Sometimes, through the window which opens on the garden,
a gust of music wafts up from Chopin at work.
All this mingles with the songs of nightingales
and the fragrance of roses."

EUGENE DELACROIX, 1842.

Acknowledgments

I would like to offer my deepest condolences to those that aided in the creation of the following weird tale. First of all, if it wasn't for Edgar A. Poe and Howard Phillips Lovecraft, the originators of the weird tale, I would not be typing these words, nor would I be as sane as I am at this late date in my life which has expressed its share of difficulties, disasters, and miseries. I would also like to thank Mrs. Fitzpatrick, my tenth-grade English teacher that awarded me with a simple ribbon of red for being the most well-read student in her class. Also, I would like to acknowledge the position that music has played in my life, for without it, I would be a hopeless slob living on the street with heroin coursing through my veins. Lastly, I should mention Mr. Ben Ohmart, the owner/creator of Bear Manor Media publishing, for having the guts to print this "manifesto" in the first place.

A Simple Prelude

I think it is vitally important to mention that this novella should be read while listening to Chopin's complete set of preludes or, if this isn't possible, any selection or grouping of musical compositions (his waltzes would do just fine) by this great Romantic composer who in my estimation was far ahead of his time. My reason for saying this is because music enriches the written word by conjuring up images that are often quite satisfying or extremely distressing. For myself, every time I read something regardless of what it might be, I hear music in my head (I am after all a musician!). My only explanation for this phenomenon is due to the fact that I've attended thousands of concerts over the last fifty years, ranging from traditional jazz to full-blown hard rock/heavy metal and electronic realizations, and that I was fortunate enough to personally meet some of the greatest musicians that ever jammed on this planet.

In the end, I'm certain that people with much more intelligence than this writer will agree that music is the Voice of the Universe. Although Frederic Chopin was only thirty-nine years old when he died in 1849 (ten days after Edgar A. Poe on October 7th), his musical legacy is on solid ground and as a musician belongs in the Pantheon of the Greats that have passed their way into the realms of the unknown. I would also like to make note that this tale is a work of pure fiction and that if it happens to resemble someone in real life, then the author expresses his condolences to those who knew such a crazy son of a bitch.

Frederic Chopin, circa 1845.

Movement No. 1

I guess the iron-framed bed beneath my ass is not so bad; in fact, it could be a lot worse, considering that the spaces between the black iron bars set in Vermont granite about three feet away from my face provides an excellent view of the interior of Sing-Sing prison, the maximum security facility operated by the New York State Department of Corrections and located in the small village of Ossining on the east bank of the beautiful Hudson River. Opened for business in October of 1826, the official legal "killers" of Sing-Sing prison, as of 1953, have executed more than five hundred individuals for a variety of crimes against humanity, such as kidnapping, bank robbery, rape, and cold-blooded murder. The food here is not too shabby, and I get to take a hot shower twice a week with a change of clothes (black and white pin strips) once a week. My next-door cellmate, Maxie Sullivan, is scheduled to be electrocuted in ten days for murdering his mother whom he says was a vile cunt with a temper as hot as a blast furnace.

Overall, he's not a bad person, but he just made some horrible decisions during his thirty-odd years on this fucked-up planet. My only true regret is that I'm not allowed to listen to the music of Frederic Chopin, only the trashy gospel music that's pumped through the mono speaker system way up in the mess hall during breakfast, lunch, and dinner. Thus, with all of this fresh in your mind, I would like to tell you how I ended up here at Sing-Sing prison before those nice prison guards in gray unlock my jail cell and haul me away for my appointment with "Old Sparky," otherwise known as "The Chair," wired with 20,000 volts of electricity.

I have no doubt whatsoever, not one single doubt, that if Frederic Chopin had managed to survive beyond the age of thirty-nine, his musical abilities would not have increased, meaning that his amazing talent for creating some of the most beautiful music of all time was intact at birth, much like Mozart. I also have no fucking doubt that the life of a special person like Chopin can only be appreciated by acknowledging what he managed to accomplished as an often physically sick person whose life was brief and full of pain. Yet despite this fact, Chopin did not fail to achieve his overarching purpose which was to bring musical rapture to a violent and fucked-up world. Of course, as is the social tendency of so-called civilized man, Chopin was often derided and ridiculed for being different and for his need to disassociate himself from his fellow human beings, most of whom were nothing more than worthless cocksuckers.

I also firmly believe that Chopin's predominant purpose in life was to create something of exquisite and long-lasting beauty and to set himself apart from commonality. If any human being within the last two hundred years managed to accomplish this rather lofty goal, it has to be Frederic Chopin. As for myself, I too had a rather lofty goal related to one of the vilest acts ever conceived by man, namely, premeditated murder, with the victim being my wife Dolores, the evilest cunt bitch of all time who certainly deserved to have her throat slashed and her body fed to a congregation of hungry alligators in Dr. Frankenstein's basement.

But unfortunately, I didn't have a congregation of alligators wallowing about in a dungeon beneath my house, so I was forced to come up with another solution for her death so I could relax and play my favorite musical composition by the great Chopin, his Prelude, Op. 28, No. 24 in D minor without being disturbed by that soulless cunt who would have burned down Carnegie Hall because she didn't like the color of the front entrance doors.

Before I begin to describe the process that I followed in order to murder my wife and hopefully get away with it, I would first like to relate a brief history of what I consider as Chopin's most outstanding piano composition. Some of the greatest musical minds of the twentieth century have called Prelude, Op. 28, No. 24 in D minor the ultimate pearl of Chopin's piano works, a natural gemstone of great beauty with haunting coloration that remains in the mind of the listener long after hearing it for the first time. This prelude is generally accepted by scholars as having been composed while Chopin was visiting Majorca, the largest island in the Balearic group off the coast of Spain in the wine-dark sea known as the Mediterranean. Chopin's friend and associate Robert Schumann once referred to this short burst of musical energy as a cannon buried in a huge flowerbed and its composer as a bold and proud musician who composed poetry with musical notes instead of words.

Novelist George Sand, also known as Amantine Lucile Dupin (no relation to Poe's Auguste Dupin, I believe), observed that this prelude forces the human soul into a terrifying manic depression which Chopin may have experienced himself while performing it for a small but dedicated audience. Technically, this piece of music could be considered as a rhapsody because it is free-flowing and spontaneous. It is also scored by Chopin as an "allegro appassionato" or something meant to be played with a great amount of emotion. Believe me, this "appassionato" was present in my mind and heart when I decided to take the life of that cunt bitch Dolores without the benefit of a congregation of hungry alligators.

At least in my musical mind, this particular prelude is highly remarkable because of its improvisational nature and ability to create a feeling of deep melancholia in the listener. Melancholia is, after all, one of the most necessary emotions required to commit murder. For the musician, melancholia throbs and pulsates with every beat of his heart. An anonymous musical reviewer once proclaimed that anyone who can play this particular prelude in a finished manner without making a single error in hitting the wrong key (all bragging aside, I count myself among those so gifted) can congratulate himself on having scaled the highest apex that a pianist can attain. Once again, the great Robert Schumann referred to Prelude, Op. 28, No. 24 in D minor as a paradigm overflowing with bold and creative forces that are striking and powerful, especially when played in a darkened room with the light of the afternoon sun barely emerging through a narrow divide in a set of black curtains.

In my humble opinion, as a rather accomplished pianist which my fucked-up wife never acknowledged to herself or our friends and relatives and who believed until the day she died that my talent was nothing but a filthy black lie, this prelude is undoubtedly one of the greatest artistic outbursts in the history of the piano as a musical instrument, a composition that burns with rage and prompts the listener to think of acts of malevolence, almost as if under the spell of a powerful stimulant like opium that creates unbounded courage and eliminates fear related to committing murder. In other words, this stimulant in the form of Chopin's Prelude in D minor removes all concerns over getting caught by the authorities and allows the killer to focus on the act itself until he reaches the point of perfection.

One method which I personally found to be of great service was to sit in a comfortable chair listening to Chopin's music through a set of headphones plugged into an amplified reel-to-reel tape recorder with the prelude recorded over and over again in an endless repetition of aural stimulation. I recall many times when my head was so full of horrendous images that I felt like running out to the street while swishing around a rusty straight razor and slicing the faces of people that happened to come within my reach.

I imagine that now would be an excellent time to reveal how my bitch wife Dolores felt about Chopin. Please try to remember that what follows are the observations of a despicable cunt that I married some twenty miserable years ago just before the beginning of World War Two when the world was thrown into chaos because of the actions of a fucking madman named Adolf Hitler. The crux of my wife's hatred for Chopin had absolutely nothing to do with his music which, by the way, she also abhorred, often calling it pure sentimental trash and the musical ravings of a perverted child. Her real hatred was for the previously mentioned George Sand, born as a female on July 1, 1804 in Paris, France. Also, please remember that the words provided below are from that cunt bitch's personal diary which I managed to steal one night after she drank too many vodka martinis and passed out on the living room couch where I fucked her in the ass without her consent:

"July 24. Paid a visit to the Wellington Public Library today. My husband Carl's unnatural obsession with Frederic Chopin has forced me to find out as much as I can about this so-called "musical genius" who is slowly destroying our marriage and my sanity. Carl knows exactly how I feel about his "idol," but I really didn't know the facts, so after glancing through some current romance novels, I went to the biography section and found a book called *The Strange Life of George Sand*, written in 1920 by Alexander Knox, a former professor of literature at Harvard University.

According to Professor Knox, when Chopin first met this fucking bitch, he allegedly confessed to a friend that he had made the acquaintance of a Parisian celebrity and found her face to be quite unattractive, if not downright frightening and repellent. From what I have gathered, Sand looked like a man who attempted to cover her ugliness with caked-on cosmetics and a fancy wig. In 1837, Chopin was persuaded by Franz Liszt, another of those Romantic pantywaists, to meet up with Sand. As Chopin allegedly relates, while sitting at a piano owned by a wealthy benefactor, he began to improvise and soon noticed the aroma of violets in the air. When he finished playing, he looked up and saw a strange "woman" leaning on the piano, gazing at him like an orangutan with a hard-on.

The "lady" in question turned out to be Sand who smiled and complemented Chopin on his playing abilities (what a dumb bitch!). The attraction of Sand to Chopin was quite powerful. At the age of thirty-seven, I guess Chopin was a rather handsome man who naturally drew in the sleazy ladies when he performed for small audiences, but what I find so infuriating and disgusting is that Chopin has been described as slim and fragile like a young woman as contrasted with the bitch whom Liszt describes as being like an Amazon with a face that would melt the heart of a chimpanzee. Also, an anonymous writer from the mid-nineteenth century declares that Sand was afflicted with nympholepsy, or that her sexual appetite bordered on a malignant disease. I would imagine that Chopin went to bed on many nights with his dick smelling like turpentine.

This could be due to the fact that her mother was a prostitute who probably fucked her clients while her weird daughter peeked through a partially closed bedroom door. I can just imagine what this weird daughter did to herself while watching her mother, frigging her own little pussy until it exploded. Not so much as an afterthought, French author and poet Charles Baudelaire whom I also abhor as a liberal son of a bitch, had this to say about Sand and Chopin who willingly stayed and got laid in her company: "The fact that there are men who could become enamored of this slut is indeed proof of the abasement of men of this generation." After analyzing an old steel engraving of Sand in the above-mentioned biography, I must admit that Baudelaire's description is quite accurate. Sand was one ugly fucking whore.

To make things more than obvious, Sand was accustomed to smoking cigars and often told those in attendance at soirees that she despised all moral restraints and basically thought that if a man can do something in public, then so can she without being chastised for it. In many ways, Sand was one of the first of those fucking disgusting feminists that see themselves as superior to men and God. Finally, Chopin admitted to Liszt that Sand was repellent and then asked if she was a real woman, an indication that he thought she might be a man in disguise.

Nonetheless, Chopin and Sand developed a close, sickening friendship which by the winter of 1838 included some kind of a sexual relationship. Maybe Chopin was gay or bisexual, a closet queen as the old saying goes in Greenwich Village. Maybe my husband Carl is a closet queen, a filthy, perverted piano player just like his idol, Frederic 'Closet Queen' Chopin. Maybe all artists are closet queens that practice sick sexual perversions that make me want to go to the nearest gun shop and buy a .44 Magnum so I can blow their fucking heads off."

There's much more like this in Dolores' diary, so maybe now you might understand why I murdered that cunt wife Dolores, a true and honest, soulless bitch. It was obvious to me then as it is now that Dolores' hatred for Chopin was so overwhelming that I believe she would've done almost anything to disrupt my passionate feelings for this giant of Western music.

In fact, I'm convinced that she thought more than once about taking a well-oiled chainsaw to the one thing in my life that I treasured above everything else, being my beautiful and extremely rare black enameled Pleyel grand piano, built in France around 1839.

Although I had no proof or provenance (or reliable documentation) that Chopin actually played this piano, it was still valued on the open market at about $750,000. I am also quite certain that if Dolores had been given the opportunity that she would have sold my Pleyel grand piano to the highest bidder at an auction in New York City and then used the money to buy a small house in the Hamptons or go on a shopping spree in Midtown Manhattan while tipping the cabbies a hundred dollars apiece. Just thinking about this makes me extremely happy to know that I was lucky enough to stumble across an unexpected way to kill that cunt bitch and rid the world of her presence once and for all.

I should mention that my initial interest in the music of Frederic Chopin began when I was still a young man. At this time, my uncle Don, a radio repairman and a bumbling alcoholic who put gin in his bacon and eggs for breakfast, gave my father a rather expensive RCA radio with big glass tubes and a tuning dial the size of a dinner plate. On many nights, I listened to "wireless" broadcasts by the New York Philharmonic and often heard works by Chopin and other Romantic composers. Later on, when my uncle Don had progressed to repairing televisions while he was drunk, my father bought an early RCA black and white set with an oval cathode ray tube or screen about five inches in diameter that allowed us to watch real broadcasts of the Philharmonic from New York City. Some years later and after getting married to that cunt bitch, I became interested in electronics and proudly owned one of the first reel-to-reel tape recorders along with a collection of taped music.

By the 1950's, I was able to purchase a state-of-the-art television, a black and white set with three Bakelite knobs; one for volume, one for brightness/contrast, and one as a channel selector. I believe it was channel nine from Windsor, Canada that was showing *The Picture of Dorian Gray*, the 1945 version with Hurd Hatfield as Gray and the beautiful Angela Lansbury as the tragic Sibyl Vane. In one scene, Dorian/Hatfield sits down at an old upright piano in a tavern and plays Prelude, Op. 28, No. 24 in D minor (he refers to it as "Prelude"). When Gray finishes playing the piece, Sibyl Vane enquires about the composer. "It's wonderful," she says. "Did you write it?" whereby Gray replies, "Frederic Chopin wrote it for a woman he loved. Her name was George Sand." For Sibyl Vane, best-known at the tavern for her rendition of "Little Yellowbird," this was a moment of enlightenment, a moment when her heart fluttered like the tiny wings of the little yellow bird that nested in her straw hat.

Sibyl observes that the piece is "full of emotion but not happy." Later in Gray's magnificent home in Mayfair, he plays the same prelude on what appears to be a Bauza piano. This turns out to be Sibyl Vane's swan song, for she commits suicide after sleeping with Gray who initially tested her morals by asking her to spend the night. After all, it is Late Victorian London and a proper woman will not have sex with a man that is not her husband unless she happens to be a whore. But Sibyl Vane is not a slut, despite being a singer in a working-class drinking venue. Oddly enough, the character of Lord Henry Wotton, an immoral Victorian asshole who goads Gray into living the life of a hedonist, is performed by veteran actor George Sand(ers).

This fine movie served as my inspiration to discover what brand of piano was most closely associated with Chopin during his lifetime. Turned out to be Pleyel, although some scholars point out that Chopin's first *real* piano was built by Juan Bauza of Palma, the capitol of the Spanish island of Mallorca. Whether Dorian Gray had a Pleyel piano in his parlor with the sheet music for "Les Preludes" is not known, but Pleyel was the true brand of choice for Chopin. According to my researches, Ignaz Joseph Pleyel was born in Lower Austria in 1757 and his musical talent became obvious when he was a mere child. In 1774, a wealthy Austrian patron arranged for Pleyel to study under Franz Joseph Haydn in musical composition, and in 1783, Pleyel became the Capellmeister or the "Master of the Choir" at Strasbourg Cathedral.

During the French Revolution of 1789 (how I have often wished that I could have been there to watch the heads roll!), Pleyel was denounced at the height of Robespierre's Reign of Terror as an enemy of the Republic, but he managed to clear his good name and subsequently settled in Paris as a seller of sheet music. In 1807, Pleyel founded his pianoforte factory, where he built some of the finest pianos in Western Europe. As a matter of historical record, Chopin made his musical debut in Pleyel's demonstration rooms in 1831 where he immediately noticed the instrument's special singing tone. Pleyel was undoubtedly pleased with this, considering that Chopin went on to become one of Europe's most highly-respected musicians of the early nineteenth century.

As to my own piano playing abilities, my parents noticed early on during my childhood that I possessed an ear for music. Since my mother and father were both great lovers of music, there was always something playing in our house, whether a radio tuned to a popular classical music station or my father attempting to play the music of Bach or Beethoven on an old German-made violin bought at a pawn shop. My first musical instrument was a classical guitar which my mother chose because of my love for the great Andres Segovia. I then moved up to a cello and attempted to emulate Pablo Casals.

In 1925, my parents and I travelled to the beautiful city of Paris, where I was first introduced to the piano through a wealthy great aunt who just happened to own the above-mentioned Pleyel grand piano. This great aunt was so impressed by my playing abilities that she promised upon her death that I would inherit the Pleyel piano. When she died five years later, the magnificent Pleyel piano was sent all the way from France to my parent's small house in Riverdale, a middle to upper-class neighborhood in the Bronx. It was here that I perfected my abilities to play the difficult music of Chopin while my mother and father provided all the love and support required in my pursuit to master the solid ivory keyboard of the magnificent Pleyel pianoforte.

I would also like to point out that my piano playing techniques and artistic interpretations were based on those of Chopin. After my parents and I arrived back in New York City following our visit to my great aunt in Paris, I began to take piano lessons in earnest from some of the most talented instructors in the city. For the most part, all of these instructors agreed that a mastery of technique was required for students like myself in order to achieve pure artistic abilities related to playing the piano. This would be in conjunction with another vital aspect, being instinct, which plays an important part in how a piece of music is played. Little did I realize how important my own instinct would become a number of years later when it came time to kill that cunt bitch known as Dolores.

I believe this would be an excellent place to explain my marriage to that cunt bitch which endured far longer than I originally anticipated. First of all, and this may sound a bit peculiar to some people, my physical appearance (I've been told that I resemble Vincent Price) had absolutely nothing to do with the attraction between myself and Dolores. It has been suggested for thousands of years that opposites attract; however, in my case, this axiom did not apply because Dolores and myself were more identical than different, at least in the beginning of our relationship. To be completely blunt about it, we were both lonely, shy, and starved for a good fucking.

However, I'm quite certain that Dolores was a virgin at the age of twenty-one, simply because of her physical awkwardness and embarrassment when I ordered her to strip her clothes off and get prepared for some hard plunging. I should mention that during this period of "sexual awakening," I had no idea of her deep-seated and unexplainable hatred for the arts. If I had, I most certainly would have told her to fuck right off and go masturbate in a closet somewhere.

After a short stint in the US Army during World War Two and with the beautiful Pleyel piano in storage, I returned home to New York City and took up residence in the boarding house of a Mrs. Greenberg, a fine-looking Jewish lady who provided much-needed financial assistance to her strangely attractive and weird niece Dolores who lived in a small apartment on the third floor of the boarding house. I call her weird because one day while strolling past her open apartment doorway, I saw her licking the furniture, especially the curved arm of a mahogany chair. I vividly recall that this apartment had a big latticed window that looked out on Gun Hill Road, so-called because during the American Revolution, some brave yet idiotic American citizens rolled a huge cannon up a hill that now lies within the boundaries of Woodlawn Cemetery and fired the cannon at the Redcoats far below. Exactly how much damage they inflicted upon the enemy is unknown.

My apartment at the boarding house was also small but comfort-able and as a British horror film fanatic once remarked about his flat in London, it was just large enough to swing a cat in it. The best part of this living space was the bathtub, a giant piece of white porcelain with eagle claw feet of brass that would've served Ed Gein perfectly for chopping up bodies. There was also a huge oil portrait of the late Mr. Greenberg, a portly man who allegedly played the piano rather well when his right hand was not wrapped around a fifth of straight Kentucky bourbon.

About three months after I moved into the boarding house, Mrs. Greenberg asked if I would be interested in having dinner with her and Dolores every Sunday night at seven o'clock and then finish up the eve-ning by watching the *Original Amateur Hour* that featured a bunch of assholes doing stupid things for a live audience. Although Mrs. Greenberg did not provide any reason for this act of domestic kindness, I became suspicious when I overheard Dolores bitching about the fact that she was all alone and was tired of not having a boyfriend or any sort of admirer. Since I was alone myself and found Dolores to be well-built in certain areas of her body (especially from the waist down), I accepted Mrs. Greenberg's offer and ended up having dinner with these two sad bitches every Sunday evening.

At these "get-togethers" in Mrs. Greenberg's well-decorated flat, I could tell almost immediately that some kind of sinister plot was being planned between her and Dolores. As it turned out, this collaboration became obvious when I began to notice that Dolores' dining chair was being moved several inches around the table and closer to where I was sitting every time I had dinner at the flat. Also, Dolores was smiling more often, an indication that she had some kind of emotional feelings for me. I assumed that she just wanted to fuck me. One evening, she showed up at dinner wearing a rather revealing dress that allowed my eyes to wander around her ample tits. It was then that I knew something was amiss, that Dolores had somehow fallen in love with me for reasons I still cannot comprehend.

About a year later, knowing full well that marriage was in my future in relation to Dolores, I went to the New York Public Library with the gigantic stone lions acting as protectors for what lies inside this massive building to consult a thin volume about thirty-fives pages in length called *Marriage,* written by Samuel Taylor Coleridge, one of the greatest literary minds of all time, subtitled "A Letter to a Young Lady" whom Coleridge does not identify. Although the date of this letter is not clear, it must have been written sometime circa 1795 when Coleridge's own marriage was falling apart. After several years of great unhappiness and the arrival of four children (some of them must have been born stoned, due to their father's addiction to laudanum), Coleridge gradually grew to detest his wife and eventually separated from her. I'm quite sure that the thought of throwing her from London Bridge and into the murkiness of the River Thames did cross his mind more than once. Here is what Coleridge has to say about that "peculiar institution" known as marriage:

"If there be one subject that should concern a young woman, both in itself and in its application to her own particular habits and circumstances, it is that of marriage; and if there be any one subject of more perplexing delicacy than any other, it is that of marriage. To both sexes, it is a state of deep and awful interest, and to enter into it without proportionate forethought is an act of folly and self-degradation. For a woman, marriage is an act tantamount to suicide, for it is a state which once entered, fills the whole sphere of a woman's moral and personal being, her enjoyments, and her duties. In the end, marriage reminds one of the disgust associated with a soiled and sordid garment that transmits a contagion once it touches the skin."

Coleridge also strikes a familiar chord by declaring that if a young woman hopes to reform the principles and personality of her husband, then she is treading on quicksand. What I found most fascinating about this letter is Coleridge's astute observation that to enter into marriage is akin to committing suicide, and that if a person (in this instance, the woman) fails to think about it beforehand, marriage is nothing more than an act based on utter stupidity, at least under most instances with few exceptions. Thus, that cunt bitch Dolores was totally unaware that she was about to step into a world of true darkness, a world inhabited by a man bent upon her absolute destruction because of her hatred for Chopin, making her a real cunt bitch and a slut.

On a sweltering August afternoon, Dolores and I were married at the Basilica of St. Patrick's Old Cathedral in Manhattan, one of those imposing stone edifices of the Catholic faith of which I do not have any affiliations. Strange as it may seem, Dolores was a practicing Catholic which should have made a positive impression on her estimations of Chopin, born as a Polish Catholic. But unfortunately, she continued to see him as a worthless son of a bitch who slept with an atheistic whore with a filthy hole between her legs. After the wedding, we headed to the Park Central Hotel on 7th Avenue, built during the Roaring Twenties when Alphonse Capone ruled Chicago as America's most cold-blooded murderer. We stayed in bed for three days, and by the spent conclusion of the third day, Dolores' virginity was a thing of the past. Let me say with all honesty that I really truly tore into her, for I recall seeing bloodspots on the sheets and the remnants of about a dozen condoms.

After our romp at the hotel, we returned to Mrs. Greenberg's boarding house where Dolores immediately moved all of her belongings into my already crowded apartment. Since my Pleyel piano was at this moment being kept at my parent's house in Riverdale, I had to be content with my collection of other instruments which I kept in a walk-in closet off the living room. This collection included two cellos (one half-size, the other one-quarter size), several violins that my parents had purchased in Paris and Vienna where they spent their honeymoon, two wonderful guitars (a 1953 Gibson L-5 Custom valued at about $17,000), and a 1946 Gibson Southern Jumbo Sunburst acoustic, and lastly, a fold-up harpsichord, made in Italy circa 1790, that played quietly and never disturbed a living soul, except for that cunt bitch who if given the opportunity would have tossed my instruments into the nearest garbage dumpster.

These fine instruments once belonged to a rich uncle from Chicago, and according to my late mother, uncle Charlie participated in the infamous St. Valentine's Day Massacre. Thus, it would seem that murder runs in my blood. I hate to admit it, but I still have the 45. caliber Thompson sub-machine gun that my uncle Charlie allegedly used in the massacre stashed away in a closet. I really don't think I'll ever need to use it, but one never knows when life is going to throw a monkey wrench in the fucking gears.

After my parents were killed in a horrible car accident in downtown Manhattan, Dolores and I moved into the house in Riverdale, where I cleaned up an old pantry in the basement in order to store the instruments that I kept at Mrs. Greenberg's boarding house. As soon as Dolores spied the magnificent Pleyel piano sitting squarely in what I called the "purple parlor" with a bronze bust of Chopin occupying a pseudo-Romanesque pedestal, her incessant bitching and complaining began in earnest.

"Why don't you get rid of that fucking thing?" she once said, or perhaps something like, "It's the ugliest thing I've ever seen. Belongs at the bottom of the Hudson River." In my mind, that was exactly where she belonged with a cinder block chained around her fucking ankles. She also despised looking at the bust of Chopin and would cover it up with an old pink pillowcase. "I just can't imagine," she would observe, "why a handsome young man like Chopin, even though he looked like a skinny girl, would sleep with that French slut who only wanted his money." When Dolores spewed out ignorant observations like this, I wanted to punch her in the face a couple of times and then throttle her with a length of barbed wire. Sometimes, my vast imagination would run wild with thoughts of cutting up her body in that big porcelain bathtub I mentioned awhile back, or stripping her naked and slowly dipping her tits in a vat of sulfuric acid.

In a short while, it became clear that Dolores was highly jealous of Frederic Chopin, simply because she knew that I was deeply in love with his music to such an extent that I was willing to spend all of my free time playing the music of a dead man instead of spending it with her, doing stupid things like shopping for clothes or figuring out what color to paint the kitchen or living room (I always preferred flat black). But I thought more than once that it was not jealousy, but pure hatred that drove Dolores to make me as miserable as possible when it came to appreciating the life and music of Chopin, such as his Preludes, Concertos, Etudes, Mazurkas, Nocturnes, Ballades, and Waltzes. I'm certain that if it was possible, Dolores would dig up the corpse of Frederic Chopin and burn it right before my eyes as she laughed triumphantly.

For some people like Dolores, the need to hate something or someone is just as powerful as the need to love or be loved. Obviously, she hated Chopin and everything to do with his genius, especially the women in his life like George Sand and the uncounted others that swooned like drugged geese whenever they heard him play. I now believe that Dolores was one of those kinds of bitches that could not live without hating someone or something. I guess it just made her feel better about herself while providing an emotional boost to her fragile, fucked-up ego.

Unlike myself, Dolores was haunted by a variety of neuroses based on an intense hatred for everything she couldn't control or change. Not long ago when she was sound asleep in her little Jenny Lind bed and I was sitting at the kitchen table with a pitcher of vodka martinis, I wrote down the following examples of her neuroses which I assume have been with her since the day she crawled out of her mother's cunt:

1. A general state of irritability. One morning, after she had consumed a bit too much red wine, Dolores complained that the carpet in the parlor was permanently damaged by the weight of the Pleyel piano, somewhere around seven hundred pounds. I suggested that we remove the carpet, whereby she complained that the finish on the oak floor would also be damaged. At this point, I casually mentioned that we could have the floor refinished. Not good enough, so she stormed outside, slammed the front door, and screamed out a litany of profanities.

2. Complaints concerning medical conditions that do not exist. Although Dolores was not medically speaking a hypochondriac, she constantly complained about ailments that troubled her in some way, such as a non-existent tumor in her head that allegedly made her go blind once in a while, or her inability to wake up from a sound sleep, even when someone slapped her straight across the fucking face which usually turned out to be yours truly. I must admit that I thoroughly enjoyed slapping her on several occasions and wanted to do other things to bring her pain and suffering like taking a cold electric clothes iron, place it on her naked stomach, plug the iron in the wall, turn the heat setting all the way up, and walk away.

3. Emotional distress related to events that normally occur during the course of one's life. For instance, Dolores would become quite upset when she switched on a lamp and the bulb would suddenly burn out, or placed the wrong shoe on the wrong foot, making it necessary to remove her shoes and start over. This was especially upsetting when the shoes were equipped with buckles or zippers. Dolores also absolutely despised the idea of cooking, particularly when it was necessary to use a gas oven. How I wished so many

times that she would've stuck her head in the oven instead of a ham or a roasting chicken.

4. Odd behaviors associated with personal guilt. Not too long ago, Dolores told one of the neighbors that their dog was keeping her awake at night with its incessant barking and howling. However, this particular neighbor did not own a dog of any kind, and when Dolores discovered this fact, she went straight to the grocery store, bought a can of dogfood, and ate it while slurping down a chocolate milkshake.

5. An uncontrollable dependency on other people and their opinions. Just the other day, Dolores was talking to our local grocer who sold us the vegetables and fruit that we kept in the house. At some point, the grocer mentioned that the tomatoes in her store were not up to par with those she had bought before from another produce company. Although there was nothing inherently wrong with these tomatoes, Dolores automatically assumed that they were poisoned with pesticides which prompted her to toss the tomatoes in the garbage.

6. Envious behavior. There is no need to clarify this trait because it flows directly from the Pleyel piano. You see, Dolores was envious of the instrument because it brought me great pleasure and contentment. Also, when I happened to be playing one of my other instruments, such as the 1953 Gibson L-5 Custom guitar, she would hurry to a window, slide it open, and allow the sound of our neighbor's lawn mower to overwhelm the guitar. When this happened, I put the guitar away and conjured up images of her head being sliced and diced under the rotating blades of the lawn mower. At one point, I considered buying a loud Fender amplifier so I could block out the roar of the lawn mower and drive her totally insane with the hum and distortion of the tubes.

7. Panic related to non-threatening situations. Yesterday afternoon, Dolores was slicing some homemade bread when she accidentally cut her finger. The screams that issued from her mouth made me think that she had cut her finger off (how pleasant it would've been if she had cut her throat). I ran into the kitchen, examined the wound, and shrugged it off, telling her that it was nothing to

be concerned about, but she panicked and insisted that I take her to the hospital for stitches. When I refused, she started throwing plates and cooking utensils at me, screaming that I didn't care if she bled to death (actually, I didn't give a shit). It would have been nice to watch her bleed to death, squirting blood all over the floor until she collapsed in a pool of scarlet slipperiness.

About a week later, following her neurotic reaction to cutting herself, I found some free time to sit alone in the little garden just outside of our kitchen. Since I was quite familiar with Chopin's love of the natural world, I attempted to recreate it in this garden which separated our house from the one next door, the one without the dog. On the left side just beyond the back door, I planted several rows of violets (recall that violets were George Sands' favorite flower) and some ornamental plants like *Laurus nobilis* or common laurel, along with some greenery and vines which I hoped would add some height to the landscape once they started to grow.

On a cool day, I would sit facing the direction of the wind and draw in the exquisite fragrance of the violets which had a calming effect upon me. Of course, that fucking cunt bitch hated the garden and said some extremely nasty things about it. "I despise the smell of violets," she would say. "They remind me of that immoral slut. I'd rather smell dead fish lying on the shore at Coney Island." When Dolores talked like this, I would do everything in my power to stay seated in my chair, rather than attacking her and punching her hard in the face. But our neighbors, those nosy sons of bitches, would have called the police with me ending up in handcuffs and being dragged away to spend the night in a filthy, fucked-up jail cell.

Besides finding some respite in the garden from Dolores' constant bitching and her long list of neuroses, I also cleared out a space in the basement where I set up a bookcase and some shelves lined with books on the great composers like Beethoven, Robert Schumann, Mozart, J.S. Bach, Brahms, and others. I also added a small collection of biographies on some ephemeral composers and musicians that most people are not familiar with, such as Pachelbel (one of Bach's contemporaries), Buxtehude (Bach's teacher), Albinoni, Offenbach, Smetana, Borodin, and one of my favorite musicians Wanda Landowska, a Polish harpsichordist who considered Chopin as a human god.

According to a number of reliable sources from World War Two, Miss Landowska once owned Chopin's original Bauza piano, but when those fucked-up Nazis invaded Paris, they looted Landowska's home and confiscated everything in sight. From what I've been able to determine, the

Bauza piano, valued at around $500,000 in the 1940's, either ended up in a French tavern with drunken Nazi soldiers using it for target practice or was hauled down a shaft in a Bavarian coal mine to conceal it from the approaching Allied armies.

In addition, I included a small collection of antique books on two of my other favorite subjects, being human anatomy and the diseases of the mind. I also set up a state-of-the-art music system with a high wattage Marantz amplifier and tuner, a Fisher turntable, and a set of Klipsch speakers rated at three hundred watts each, more than enough to blow the cinder block walls out and keep Dolores in a state of glorious mental agitation.

Here I often sat for hours on an old red upholstered chair, absorbed in a biography about the life and tragic circumstances of one of my favorite composers or musicians. Once in a while, that vile cunt bitch would slither down the stairs and simply stand in front of me while shaking her head, acting as though I was doing something totally immoral like cutting up a dead body in the cement sink next to the Maytag washer, or drowning my first-born son (God forbid!) in the laundry tub full of scalding hot water.

While perusing a book written more than a hundred years ago by an author no one has ever heard of, I came across a rather interesting quote attributed to Landowska, the oft-quoted "Mistress of the Harpsichord." In June of 1894 some twenty years before the outbreak of the First World War, Landowska must have been deep in thought concerning Chopin, for she declares with the awe of a painter who has just laid down the final brushstrokes on a Flemish masterpiece, "How could I live without Chopin, whose melodies shake one's soul? His music reminds me of the pretty Polish peasant girls lingering in familiar and quaint hamlets, and of the fields and the meadows of the open Polish landscape. I stand in awe of the master and wish that I could give him my soul and my thoughts." How wonderful it would have been if Dolores had felt the same as Madam Landowska! This grand lady died in 1959 at the age of eighty, but I would have rather had her in my bed than that cunt bitch Dolores any day of the week. Much like Chopin, Landowska's favorite instrument maker was Pleyel with its double-tiered Grand Modele harpsicord made in 1927.

Alfred Cortot (1877 to 1962), one of Landowska's contemporaries, made it clear to his friends and associates that the music of Chopin created deep emotional feelings within his volcanic heart, even though he was a staunch supporter of the Nazi Occupation of France during World War Two. An accomplished transcriber of piano music composed during the Romantic Period, Cortot once referred to Prelude, Op. 28, No. 24 in

D minor as a mixture of passion, blood, and death. Of course, these three elements are the main ingredients of premeditated murder with the first symbolizing the emotional foundation of the person ready to commit homicide; the second and third are the results, with blood being the avatar of Morrigan, the Celtic deity of murder and doom, and death personified as Ankou who usually appears as a skeleton draped in a black cloak wielding a razor-sharp scythe. In essence, he is the ikon of foreknowledge in relation to approaching death.

Cortot also interpreted the conclusion of Prelude, Op. 28, No. 24 in D minor as being filled with startling imagery which following a very short and formidable silence, erupts with the dull thud of three notes, all in D minor which seem to emerge from a tomb as the marble door pivots open. From my perspective, these notes symbolize the downward thrust of a dagger as it penetrates the beating heart of a human body (the first note), is withdrawn, penetrates again (the second note), is withdrawn, and penetrates again (the third note). The blade is then withdrawn with the wound left flayed open that allows blood to erupt like a garden hose and act as a veneer on the ivory keys, slowly spreading until it drips continuously on the floor. As you might expect, the blood in this instance belongs to that cunt bitch; however, using a knife to kill someone is a very messy procedure, much like slaughtering cattle, or a surgeon disemboweling a patient to reach a diseased organ.

I know this from personal experience because during my service in the army during World War Two at the famous Battle of the Bulge, I was forced to run a bayonet through the abdomen of a young German soldier standing about two feet in front of me. His blood gushed out in spurts like squeezing a balloon filled with water. Of course, my uniform was ruined and it took several hours to wash the dried-up blood from my hands. Afterwards, I felt the strangest satisfaction in knowing that I had disemboweled that son of a bitch and that his filthy Nazi mother would never see her son again.

When I had finally made up my mind to murder Dolores, it took a long time and a lot of hard thinking to come up with a way to carry out my plans. Amazingly, while taking a nice hot shower, the answer came to me like a flash of intuitive improvisation. One other area that I have long held dear to my heart is the cinema which of course Dolores considered as a complete waste of time. Along with owning the Pleyel piano and the other instruments I mentioned earlier, I also had a large collection of movies that I stored in a spare room in the basement with the glass block windows painted flat black. All of these movies were reel-to-reel acetate copies that tended to rot away if kept in an environment of heat and moisture. So, in order to prevent this from happening, I installed an air conditioner in the spare room that ran twenty-four hours a day. This drove Dolores insane, always bitching that I was wasting money on electricity that could be better used for watching one of those stupid TV programs that did nothing but rot the brain of the viewer.

All of these movies have one thing in common. They belong to a genre known as *film noir* or "dark film." Most scholars agree that films that fall within this genre share a number of common elements related to directorial style, atmosphere, character development (or the lack of it), timeframe (late 1940's to mid-1950's), and subject matter which in most instances involves some type of crime with premeditated murder at the top of the list. Also, these "dark films" feature instances of violent death and brutality, such as being shot at point-blank range, repetitive stabbings, strangulation, poisoning, and good old-fashioned beatings with a club or some kind of blunt object. In essence, as French critics have noted, *film noir* are celluloid adventures steeped in death.

What I decided to do was to view some of my favorite "dark films" that contained themes and motifs related to murder and mayhem with the basic goal to discover which method of murder best met my immediate needs. It pains me to admit it, but I felt that Dolores deserved to be killed by the most atrocious means available but in such a way that it would not leave behind any sort of indication or forensic evidence that a second party (being myself) was involved in the act. All I can say at this point is that the method or "modus operandi" had to be unique, and please remember that I had no desire to be remembered as an infamous killer. However, it would have been fine by me to have had Norman Bates as my closest friend and associate.

Some may say that Dolores was simply overloaded with eccentricities or that she exhibited whimsical behavior that deviated from what some consider as 'normal.' However, she was not eccentric; she was not a whimsical person; and she was not by any stretch of the imagination a normal person. Thus, after twenty-five miserable years of marriage, I decided to kill her. Such a decision, I felt, was not so bad, considering that my motives were far better than those of Mr. Albert Fish, one of the most notorious killers of all time who bragged to the New York City police in the mid 1920's that God had told him to murder, mutilate, and consume children. I read somewhere that Fish was known to have kept strips of fleshy young buttocks in his icebox sealed in Ball Mason jars. Fish was duly executed at Sing-Sing prison in 1936 after being strapped in "Old

Sparky." I wonder if the prison guards had any part of him for dinner? As for Dolores, all I can say at this point is that I swore to do my utmost best to see that she experienced all the damnations of Hell. Chopin and that alleged whore from Paris would certainly have been proud of me.

Well, I guess it's time for dinner here at the prison because those nice guards in gray are unlocking my cell along with dozens of others up here in Death Row. Once we arrive at the heavily-guarded little mess hall reserved for killers, I always sit with Maxie Sullivan who murdered his cantankerous mother several years ago. He often tells me some of the wildest stories I've ever heard in my life. For example, sometime in the late 1920's when Prohibition was in full swing, Maxie belonged to a gang of bootleggers and killers known as the Purple Gang that shipped crates of Seagrams whiskey from Canada across the Detroit River in barges equipped with three-inch cannon just in case the Coast Guard showed up.

As Maxie tells it, he did business with Al Capone whose organization bought Canadian whiskey (Seagrams) for his thirsty customers in Chicago. Maxie also admits that the Purple Gang was involved in the infamous Lindbergh baby kidnapping in 1932. Maxie is very proud of his connections with the old underworld and brags to anyone that will listen how the Purple Gang reigned supreme by controlling gambling, the sale and manufacture of bootleg liquor and beer, and the drug trade. But like I said before, Maxie is a nice fucking fellow and doesn't deserve a visit with "Old Sparky." Time certainly flies when you're eating and conversing with your friends. I'm back in my cell now, so I'll continue with my little story.

Movement No. 2

So as not to arouse any suspicions concerning my plans to murder that cunt bitch Dolores, I gave her a shitload of money so she could hit the town and buy whatever she wanted, no matter the cost. She was always attracted to jewelry, especially anything with diamonds (they are a girl's best friend, I guess) which made her extremely happy and contended under the assumption that these baubles would make her appear more attractive and less dowdy. I was able to do this because of my great aunt Matilda who once owned the magnificent Pleyel piano and left me her entire fortune somewhere in the area of $50 million francs when she died at the ripe old age of one hundred and three.

Fortunately, Dolores found great pleasure in hanging out with her fucked-up girlfriends and spent hours in the stores in downtown Manhattan which provided the time I needed to relax in that spare room in the basement and watch as many "dark films" as I wished without being pestered by her constant whining and bitching. I must admit that it was not an easy task to determine how many films I would have to watch before I discovered my "modus operandi" related to putting Dolores in an early grave. But as the late great author and *film noir* screenwriter Jim Thompson once quipped, "Life is a bucket of shit with a barbed wire handle," meaning that life is always ready to throw a curve ball and fuck up all your plans when you least expect it.

I began my film watching sessions on a Saturday afternoon while Dolores was visiting Mrs. Greenberg, now in her nineties, and undoubtedly showing off what she had purchased downtown with the money I had given her. Knowing that Dolores would spend the entire evening at her aunt's boarding house and not return home until at least two or three o'clock in the morning, I selected several films from my collection, made a pitcher of vodka martinis, and took a seat in that comfortable stuffed red chair that once belonged to my aunt Matilda. I repeated this exact same scenario every day while Dolores was out shopping, viewing some twenty "dark film" examples from the mid 1940's through the early

1950's as the smell of heated acetate (imagine the smell of burning film negatives in a wastebasket) circulated through the spare room amid the constant clicking of the projector.

Every so often, I would stop the film and write down some pertinent notes concerning how the main characters committed murder and their "modus operandi." After viewing these films, I gathered together a number of excellent ideas on how to go about murdering Dolores who never even suspected what I was doing in that spare room with the flat black windows, except for viewing some of my favorite cinema classics that in her idiotic opinion belonged in a bonfire. I should also mention that my fixation related to murdering that cunt bitch was greatly increased by viewing these films which created a myriad of disturbing fantasies that could only occur in a nightmare, such as how it would feel to see Dolores lying in a freshly-dug grave while wearing nothing but the skin she was born in and how delightful it would be to cut a peephole in the side of her casket and watch her body being eaten by worms.

Although it really doesn't make any difference right now, here's the list of the "dark films" that I viewed over the course of several weeks while still living at my home in Riverdale with a nice and quiet neighborhood made up of old families and single women with big tits. Some of these films are relatively well-known, while others have been confined to the dustbins of film history. What's really interesting about some of these films is that the soundtracks or musical scores are eerily similar in structure and tonality to a number of Chopin's etudes and preludes, a sign that many of the directors shared a deep love for the composer regardless of his affiliations with a filthy French whore. Come to think of it, Hollywood has introduced its share of French film actresses that started out their careers as streetwalkers on the Champ-Elysees:

> 1. *Strangers on a Train* (1951), directed by Alfred Hitchcock. Farley Granger and Robert Walker. Two strangers meet up on a train and agree to murder someone that the other stranger wants dead, being Walker's father and Granger's wife. Involves shootings and strangulation.

> 2. *Double Indemnity* (1944), directed by Billy Wilder. Fred MacMurray, Barbara Stanwyck, Edward G. Robinson. MacMurray, an insurance salesman, and Stanwyck plot to kill her husband by pushing him from a moving train for the insurance with a "double indemnity" clause.

3. *Touch of Evil* (1958), directed by Orson Welles. Charlton Heston, Orson Welles, Janet Leigh. An American building contractor is murdered when his car blows up. Involves kidnapping and police corruption.

4. *The Killers* (1946), directed by Robert Siodmak, based on a short story by Ernest Hemingway. Burt Lancaster, Ava Gardner, Edmund O'Brien. Lancaster, a former prize fighter (light heavyweight) in a motel room, waiting for thugs to show up and kill him. Also involves a beautiful and deadly "femme fatale" in the form of Ava Gardner. Dolores is in no way a "femme fatale" but she is a cunt bitch, just like Gardner in this noir classic.

5. *Key Largo* (1948), directed by John Huston. Academy Award Best Actress Claire Trevor. Humphrey Bogart, Edward G. Robinson, Lauren Bacall. World War Two vet Bogart gets caught up with gangsters at Key Largo in the Florida Keys, led by Robinson as Johnny Rocco, a stereotype of Al Capone. Lots of gunplay, roughhousing, "broad" abuse.

6. *The Postman Always Rings Twice* (1946), directed by Tay Garnett. John Garfield, Lana Turner, Cecil Kellaway. Garfield, a down-and-out drifter, conspires with Turner to kill her husband, the middle-aged owner of a roadside restaurant. Turner wants it to look like an accident which includes a whack on her husband's head while he's in the shower. A faked car accident involving alcohol goes haywire.

7. *D.O.A. (Dead on Arrival)* (1949), directed by Rudolph Mate. Edmund O'Brien, Pamela Britton. O'Brien discovers that he's been poisoned by persons unknown; no known antidote. One of the best noirs about murder by poisoning.

8. *The Naked City* (1948), directed by Jules Dassin. Barry Fitzgerald, Howard Duff, Dorothy Hart. A beautiful blonde model is found drowned in her apartment bathtub. The cops assume that it's suicide, but later discover she was murdered. A great noir drowning example.

9. *The Unfaithful* (1947), directed by Vincent Sherman. Ann Sheridan, Lew Ayres, Zachary Scott. A rich socialite kills a man,

insisting that he was an intruder/burglar (in truth, her lover). Turns out quite differently, it wasn't self-defense.

10. *Kiss of Death* (1947), directed by Henry Hathaway. Victor Mature, Coleen Gray, Richard Widmark. Mature gets caught during a jewel heist, refuses to rat on his partners in crime. He finally relents to get out of prison; Widmark as Tommy Udo is spectacular; pushes a mother in a wheelchair down a flight of stairs, grins and laughs with glee. A real sadist. Lots of gunplay.

11. *Whirlpool* (1949), directed by Otto Preminger. Gene Tierney, Richard Conte, Jose Ferrer. Tierney is a woman that suffers from kleptomania (she enjoys stealing things). Her doctor hypnotizes her as a possible cure, but she ends up at the scene of a murder with no memory concerning how she got there.

12. *Murder by Contract* (1958), directed by Irving Lerner. Vince Edwards, Hershel Bernardi, Phillip Pine. Edwards is a highly ruthless contract killer who has a problem with killing women. A classic noir "hitman" scenario.

13. *Undercurrent* (1946), directed by Vincente Minnelli. Katharine Hepburn, Robert Taylor, Robert Mitchum. Hepburn plays a middle-aged spinster who later suspects her husband of being a psychotic killer with plans to murder her. Dolores is not a spinster and I'm certainly not a psychotic killer.

14. *The Scarlet Claw* (1944), directed by Roy William Neill. Based on characters created by Sir Arthur Conan Doyle. Basil Rathbone, Nigel Bruce, Gerald Hamer. Sherlock Holmes (Rathbone) investigates a murder allegedly committed by a supernatural monster. Supernatural, indeed!

15. *The Sniper* (1952), directed by Edward Dmytryk. Arthur Franz, Adolphe Menjou, Gerald Mohr. Story of a mysterious sniper who only kills brunettes. By sheer coincidence, Dolores was a brunette in her youth.

16. *Deception* (1946), directed by Irving Rapper. Bette Davis, Paul Henreid, Claude Rains. A piano teacher believes her fiancé has

been killed in World War Two. In fact, he survived and returns to her. Davis's new love is jealous and decides to throw a monkey wrench in the gears. First noir to my knowledge that involves pianos!

17. *Possessed* (1947), directed by Curtis Bernhardt. Joan Crawford, Van Heflin, Raymond Massey. Crawford plays a woman with catalepsy who ends up in a psychiatric hospital. Shades of Edgar Allan Poe!

18. *The Price of Fear* (1956), directed by Abner Biberman. Merle Oberon, Lex Barker, Charles Drake. Barker is the co-owner of a race track who gets set up by a beautiful, dark-haired woman for a hit-and-run crime. Run Dolores over with a friend's car?

19. *They Made Me a Criminal* (1939), directed by Busby Berkeley. John Garfield, Claude Rains, the Dead End Kids. Garfield as a boxer who gets framed for murder by killing someone with his car while drunk. Dolores loves vodka martinis and she can't drive worth a shit.

20. *The Mystery of Marie Roget* (1942), directed by Phil Rosen. Based on the short story by Edgar Allan Poe. Patric Knowles, Maria Montez, Maria Ouspenskaya. Knowles as detective Dupin attempts to solve the murder of Marie Roget. In Poe's original story, Roget is Mary Rodgers who drowned in the Hudson River under mysterious circumstances. Oddly, Poe's answer to the alleged true crime turned out to be dead-on accurate years after the story was published.

Out of these films, I had twenty excellent choices at my disposal with a few overlapping in regards to a methodology that I could utilize to end the life of that cunt bitch named Dolores. In no particular order of usefulness: 1), buy a gun from a lowlife addicted to heroin and shoot the bitch without being suspected of the crime; 2), push or dump her from some type of moving conveyance like a train or the subway; 3), buy her a brand-new Mercedes and blow it up with a bomb planted underneath it; 4), hire a "femme fatale" or another woman to kill her. Some old bar hag would do nicely; 5), place Dolores "in the wrong place at the wrong time" so that a gang of thugs can rape and kill her (plenty in the Bronx);

6), whack her in the head with a cotton sock full of marbles while she's in the shower or smash a fifth of whiskey over her head while she's driving, jump out of the car, and make it look like she slammed into a tree while intoxicated; 7), buy some lethal poison and put it in her coffee or orange juice; 8), drown her in the bathtub after she's drank a pitcher of vodka martinis; 9), make it look like someone broke into the house and killed her during a burglary; 10), push her down the basement stairs and make it look like an accident; 11), hypnotize her and make her think that she killed someone, thus sending her to prison for life without parole; 12), hire a paid assassin (preferably an Irish gangster) to kill her; 13), pretend that I'm a crazy son of a bitch and accidentally kill her with a claw hammer; 14), convince the police that Dolores was killed by a strange supernatural monster (New York City is full of such things); 15), hire a sniper to shoot her through the bedroom window in broad daylight; 16), fake my own death, then come back and kill her (I really like this one!); 17), make the authorities think that Dolores is insane and have her put in an asylum where hopefully an inmate will kill her; 18), run her over with my Jaguar and speed away without being seen; 19), get her drunk and tell her to go to the store for more booze (liked I said, Dolores is a really bad driver); and 20), and last but not least, take her on a sightseeing tour of the beautiful Hudson River, strangle her with a red silk scarf, and dump her naked body in the river during a moonless night. I could buy an Edgar Allan Poe mask just to be on the safe side.

Earlier today, one of the nice guards here at the prison brought me an old cardboard box plastered with a label of a can of Stoker's green beans. This was quite unusual because prisoners on Death Row are not allowed to have very many personal belongings.

"The warden said it would be alright for you to have this," said the guard while opening my jail cell door. "There's no dirty magazines in it if that's what you're thinking." The guard slid the box over by my feet, then closed the jail cell door. As I started searching through the box, I came across something I had long forgotten about, a strange little short story that I wrote many years before meeting that slut whore Dolores. In my youth, I prided myself on my musical abilities, but I also had a great interest in weird fiction and the twisted shit of Charlie Bukowski and William S. Burroughs who once enlightened us by stating "Nothing is true, everything is permitted," thus making it allowable to murder anyone you wish. Personally, I found Bukowski's legendary drunkenness to be somewhat upsetting, simply because I was unable to write a single word when stoned or inebriated with vodka martinis. So, here's my little tale. I hope it doesn't make you want to call me a fucking misogynist because truthfully, I love pussy.

"Compulsion"

"After working for ten long years for Mr. Andiron, the famous New York City shirtmaker, poor Daphne's will to live had been sapped almost entirely away. If her cheeks had remained like puffy donuts with pink frosting, and if her beautiful eyes had remained full of life like light brown andalusites, she might have remained as an extremely attractive and lively girl. Nonetheless, Daphne always tried to keep her shoulders and back straight, for she knew that because of her wearisome work, the beauty of her figure was slowly fading away as was her waist from eating too many pastries from the bakery just around the corner from the factory. Most of the men that worked and sweated in this horrible place were allowed to wear sleeveless undershirts, once sparkling white but now dingy and yellowed from the incessant dust in the air (Mr. Andiron did not believe in air conditioning nor proper ventilation). But unlike the men, the women were ordered by Mr. Andiron to tuck their heavy blue work shirts into their skirts (no pants allowed) and keep their sleeves rolled up no further than the elbow which allowed their bare arms to dangle about like the necks of dead swans.

After toiling year after year in this hothouse of misery, poor Daphne was beginning to look her age. Her neck was full of wrinkles that shouldn't be there, and her hands were like those of a mummy, dried out as if bathed in too much natron. But Daphne's mind was still sharp and clear, for she constantly dreamed of owning her own home in the suburbs, and having several clean children dangling about her knees as she stood at the stove cooking dinner. But unlike the other women at the factory, Daphne's face remained expressionless at seven o'clock in the evening when the piano music of Frederic Chopin stimulated the oval transducers hanging in each corner of the shop, pointing down like innocuous gargoyles far above the stone pavement of Notre Dame. This meant that it was time for the ladies to pack up their belongings and head for home, where they would suffer at the hands of their brutish husbands, all except Daphne who kept to her work past quitting time, ironing a crumpled stack of white shirts until they were wrinkle-free like the sheets on a four-masted schooner.

Out of sheer boredom, Daphne glanced across the workroom and smiled as best as she could at Ben Donahee who had just finished inspecting a pile of freshly-ironed white shirts. For a brief moment, Ben smiled back, thinking in his little warped mind what Daphne would look like if she was stripped naked and leaning over a work table with her plump ass up in the air. But the piano music of Chopin continued to wobble through the oval transducers which meant that Daphne had to leave work and go to her spartan apartment in the Bronx. She would have to go all alone, as usual, because Ben Donahee had no intention of asking her for a date because he knew in his perverted soul that she would never consent to a night of wild, uninhibited sex. As far as he was concerned, Daphne was probably a stone-cold bitch like most of the women he knew and probably was a virgin at the age of thirty-five.

But unknown to Ben, Daphne possessed a deep-seated compulsion to see herself and Ben Donahee romping stark naked in a freshly-laundered bed with red satin sheets and pillowcases. Since Daphne knew that Ben was a great admirer of Miss Wanda Jackson, the "Queen of Rockabilly," she had managed to squirrel away some money to buy a complete set of Jackson's rockabilly hits from the 1950's on black vinyl which she intended to play on an old monaural record player while having sex with Ben, hoping that his penis was sufficiently large enough to fulfill her desires. With these thoughts and a few others circuiting through her brain, Daphne smiled once again at Ben but this time a bit more pleasantly, hoping that he would respond before leaving his station at the table and heading for his apartment on Kingsbridge Road in Fordham, just a few steps from Edgar Poe's dilapidated white cottage. But unfortunately, Ben did not respond in the way she had wished. He simply turned around, slipped on a blue cotton jacket, and hurried away, exiting through a set of steel doors and into the dimming sunlight on Bleeker Street.

When Daphne arrived home about an hour later, and after hanging her coat on a hook on the backside of the apartment door, she sat down at a small writing desk, opened a drawer, and removed a diary with a bright green cover decorated with yellow daisies. "What should I write today?" she thought while opening the diary and picking up a sharpened yellow pencil. As soon as the black lead in the pencil touched one of the pages in the diary, Daphne wrote "Today, Ben Donahee spurned me, so I've decided to kill him. Not sure how I'm gonna do it, but I'll think of something." Daphne closed her diary and did nothing for about five minutes. She then opened another drawer in the small writing table. Her hazel brown eyes pivoted slightly and glanced inside the open drawer. She then inserted her right hand, removing a German-made Walther PPK-L pistol, 7.65 mm. which her late uncle Joe had told her was the original pistol used by Adolf Hitler to kill himself in his Fuhrerbunker on April 30, 1945. She had only fired the pistol once in her life, but was planning on firing it at least one more time to kill Ben Donahee as he stood in his sleeveless white undershirt at his table at Mr. Andiron's shirt factory sometime around seven A.M. the very next morning which happened to be a Friday.

Daphne opened her diary to the exact same page as before and wrote, "I have decided to kill Ben Donahee with Hitler's own pistol. I realize that I'll probably end up in prison for the rest of my life, but that's alright. I have nothing to live for anyways except more misery, sweat, and toil in Mr. Andiron's fucked-up shirt factory." As if the fingers of Satan had seized her by the chin, forcing her to gaze up at a calendar hanging on the wall, Daphne noticed that the date was Thursday, April 29th, one day before Hitler's "deathday." For some odd reason, Daphne bundled together all of the black vinyl LP's of Wanda Jackson's rockabilly music and dropped them from a wide-open bedroom window some five stories above an alley lined with garbage cans. The monaural record player soon followed Miss Jackson's albums, and when they connected with the pavement, an echo of immense proportions rose up as did a shabbily-dressed bum with a jug of wine.

"Hey, ya fuckin' bitch!" hollered up the bum. "Ya almost killed me!"

The bum staggered under the weight of the jug of wine, then fell hard against the brick wall of the apartment building. Daphne smiled leisurely at the bum and quickly closed the bedroom window.

Friday, April 30th. 7 A.M. on the nose. The double set of steel doors pivoted open, and Daphne strolled right past Ben Donahee who always arrived five minutes early at the factory, standing at his work table, waiting for another pile of freshly-ironed white shirts. On this bright and some-what chilly morning, Daphne was about to experience the unexpected, something so far removed from an extraordinary compulsion that she would be unable to process it in her fucked-up brain. As soon as she arrived at her work table, Daphne felt a hand on her left shoulder, thinking that it was probably Mr. Andiron with some bad news about her employment at the factory. When she turned around, Ben Donahee was standing there in his sleeveless white undershirt, holding a bouquet of red roses.

"These are for you," he said. "I thought maybe we could go out on a date or something."

"Why, thank you!" said Daphne, as several tiny teardrops rolled down her cheeks.

"Maybe we can have dinner at my place tomorrow night," suggested Ben Donahee.

"That would be great! I'll be there at eight o'clock sharp, OK?"

"That would be fine. Do you know where I live?"

"Yes, Ben, I know."

Daphne smiled at Ben as he triumphantly walked back to his work table and commenced to inspect a pile of freshly-ironed white shirts. Daphne did the same, smiling with content as she ironed some wrinkled white shirts while admiring Ben's rosy gift that complemented the whiteness of the shirts on her work table. Then her thoughts turned to that bundled-up pile of black vinyl Wanda Jackson albums that were now lying smashed on the pavement of the alley below her bedroom window. Regret was plastered all over her face as was a tinge of sorrow for the wino in the alley whose life was almost extinguished by the black vinyl LP's and the monaural record player. For the rest of the workday, a fracture of regret for the lost Wanda Jackson was etched on Daphne's face and for a fleeting moment, the image of the Walther pistol that Daphne had tucked inside the waist of her skirt just before leaving her apartment, occupied her thoughts and strengthened her compulsion.

Saturday night, May 1st. At approximately 10 P.M., Daphne had managed to fill up about five pages in her diary with her thoughts concerning her job at Mr. Andiron's shirt factory, her feelings for Ben Donahee, and his bouquet of red roses that now resided in a blue vase on a mahogany nightstand. Without giving it much thought, Daphne closed her diary, opened the drawer in her writing desk, withdrew the Walther PPK-L pistol, cocked the hammer, placed the end of the barrel in her mouth, and pulled the trigger. The eyes of the worthless wino down in the alley crept open like snake slits when he attempted to stand and tilt his head back to get a good view of Daphne's open bedroom window high overhead.

"Hey, ya stupid bitch," he hollered. "Ya woke me up!"

The bum guzzled a mouthful of cheap red wine, and in Daphne's apartment, a Persian rug imitation was soaked with blood and pieces of a cerebral cortex, and the Walther PPK-L pistol occupied Daphne's lifeless bloody hand at the end of her right arm, dangling like the neck of a dead swan."

Please don't assume that I was hoping that Dolores would kill herself like Daphne and relieve me of the responsibility for killing her. Of course, that would've been a nice gesture on her part, relieving the world and myself of her fucking presence all at the same time. As to the *film noir* scenarios, I didn't actually believe any of them would work in real life; they are, after all, slices of true American 'hard-boiled' fiction dreamed up by old-time screenwriters (or writers of "photoplays" as they used to be called) like the amazing Ben Hecht, Maxwell Anderson *(Key Largo)*, Charles Brackett *(Sunset Boulevard)*, and James M. Cain *(Double Indemnity* and *The Postman Always Rings Twice)*, all of whom looked like ordinary mid-twentieth century businessmen with thick black glasses and thin moustaches. Most of them were also consumers of popular greasy hair products that they slathered on their somewhat balding heads. Not surprisingly, many of these "photoplay" writers were multi-talented with Hecht pegged as a child prodigy with a penchant for the violin and the piano.

Therefore, in order to murder that cunt whore Dolores as cleanly as possible, I was forced to come up with other methodologies or some kind of *modus operandi* that would guarantee a life filled with complete pleasure and plenty of opportunity to play the music of Chopin until I dropped dead, preferably while sitting naked at the magnificent Pleyel piano.

Several months after viewing these and other "dark films," something truly remarkable occurred that was totally unexpected; and no, Dolores did not commit suicide like that dumb-ass Daphne in my weird tale. It was like strolling down the boulevard when all of a sudden, a chunk of concrete lands on your head and you see the proverbial light. I hope you recall my earlier observations on Dolores' fucked-up neuroses, one being her constant complaints about medical conditions that were all in her worthless mind. Please let me explain as best as I can the overall facts related to this astonishing and unexpected occurrence.

One moonless evening while reading a collection of letters written by and about Chopin in one of his biographies, I came across something penned by George Sand from the city of Barcelona in Spain to her friend the Countess Carlotta Marliani. In this letter from 1839, Sand recalls with distress that Chopin experienced a "blood-spitting fit" related to his consumptive condition that was brought on by riding in a carriage that lacked supportive springs in the under-carriage. In other words, it was a very bumpy ride for Chopin. This incident triggered the idea in my head that Chopin must surely have experienced occasional difficulties related to sleeping. Imagine waking up in the middle of the night coughing one's head off and seeing splatters of blood on the pillowcase, and then attempting to go back to sleep without fretting about the incident. Although I've been unable to locate supportive evidence, I'm convinced that Chopin must have experienced episodes of sleep deprivation which affected his attention span and ability to focus and consolidate his musical memories. His reaction time must also have been negatively affected.

What does any of this have to do with that cunt bitch Dolores? Remember what I said earlier about her occasional inability to wake up from a sound sleep? Despite the fact that we do not sleep together in the same bed (we have separate bedrooms), I happened to enter her bedroom one fateful night, looking for her diary so I could see what she had written about me. She was sound asleep, stretched out on her back and covered with a blue blanket.

At first, I thought nothing of it until I noticed that the blanket was not moving related to her breathing. I walked over to her side, pulled back the blanket, and checked her pulse. To my utter astonishment, I felt nothing, not even the faintest evidence of a heartbeat. I then placed my head directly against her chest. I heard nothing. I staggered back and practically fell in a big stuffed chair. It was just too good to be true, I thought. Is Dolores dead? My first conclusion was that she had died from a massive heart attack, but a few moments later, I saw the index finger on her right hand twitch slightly. I was completely perplexed and remained in the chair for a few minutes. Her index finger did not move again, nor did any part of her body.

I immediately headed downstairs to consult one of those antique medical books that I kept along with the biographies on famous musicians. Although I didn't possess anything on the complexities of sleep, I did have a book written in the mid 1800's concerning 'female troubles.' After scanning through the table of contents, I turned to a chapter entitled "Sleep and Sleep-Related Disorders." One of the sub-sections was called "Catalepsy." Little did I realize that this discovery would mark the beginning of the end for that cunt whore Dolores.

"Catalepsy. This affliction is extremely rare. According to a prominent American physician, catalepsy occurs chiefly in those who have weak and excitable nervous systems, feeble health, and ill-governed minds, and who may be said not to possess a healthy mind in a healthy body. As noted by Dr. Thomas Reynolds of Cambridge University, the overall symptoms include the persistence of the limbs in a state of balanced muscular contraction or a state of stiffness. The limbs can be readily moved by the observer, but they return to their former positions where they remain for hours or even days. All awareness of reality and the ability to move are lost; however, circulation and respiration remain but are also retarded to varying degrees, often to the point of apparent non-existence."

An "ill-governed mind" perfectly described that lump of shit inside Dolores' head which she used all too infrequently. "Weak and excitable" also characterized her overall central nervous system to the letter. If the very late Dr. Reynolds was correct, then I could assume that Dolores suffered from catalepsy, perhaps inherited from her schizoid parents. Come to think of it, her mother's sleeping habits (another bitch that I met a few times over the years) were somewhat unusual because it took a great deal of noise and shaking to wake her up for breakfast. I remember one day when city workers were putting up a scaffold outside of her apartment building so they could resurface the brick façade. The extreme noise caused by the workers never affected her, for she remained sound asleep, even during the noisiest part of their construction.

Once again, I paid a visit to the New York Public Library on a dismal Friday morning and did a complete search for anything I could find on catalepsy. One of the librarians that I had known for many years had never heard of this disorder, but he did direct me to a collection of old medical pamphlets held in the Manuscripts and Archives Division, where I spent more than five hours searching through at least a hundred dusty pamphlets. In one of these I found the following description, dated 1895:

"CATALEPSY. A rare medical condition in which the victim experiences the suspension of all physical sensation and movement and for all intents and purposes appears to be dead. As noted by Dr. John T. Smithson of New York University, while in a cataleptic state or suspension, every vital function like breathing and the beating of the heart is reduced to the lowest possible limit and to such a degree as to simulate actual death. Usually, this physical suspension only lasts for several hours, but in extreme instances, can endure for two or three days, or in special cases, up to four days or longer."

There were other medical pamphlets from the late 1800's that fully described the condition but no cure for it. I asked my librarian friend if I could check these pamphlets out, but because they were part of an extensive medical reference collection, they had to remain at the library. I did the next best thing by slipping the pamphlets in a coat pocket and casually walking out of the library. Of course, I had every intention of returning the pamphlets at a later date.

Upon returning home from the library and placing the pamphlets in a plain brown envelope which I then hid in a desk drawer, I found Dolores still sound asleep, so I hurried downstairs, placed an old LP of Chopin's preludes on the turntable, switched it on along with the Marantz amplifier, and sat back to think long and hard about the information I had found on catalepsy. But I was now in what some might call a quandary or a situation of perplexity related to what to do next. How the fuck could I prove beyond a reasonable doubt that Dolores suffered from catalepsy? As far as I could tell, there were no tests or examinations that would help determine the presence of this crazy disorder. I also realized that I wasn't dealing with a scenario straight out of an old *film noir* classic. The only answer to my dilemma was patience and time, meaning that I would have to wait and see if that cunt bitch happened to wake up after sleeping for more than twenty fucking hours.

After listening to Chopin's preludes for about three hours, I headed upstairs to bed, but first, I took a quick look at Dolores, still sound asleep with an ever so faint smile on her face. I glanced at a wind-up clock on her nightstand; it was past two in the morning, so I thought nothing about seeing her still sleeping comfortably. I recall that it was about two-thirty when I climbed in my own bed and attempted to forget about Dolores by thinking how pleasant it would be to see her dead and out of the way so I could spend my remaining years in peace and comfort with the music of Chopin constantly playing throughout the house.

Around ten the next morning, I crept to the door of Dolores' bedroom and slowly pushed it open. She was still sound asleep and had not apparently moved a single inch all night. The blanket was unruffled and there were no indications that she had left her bedroom during the night. I became quite excited, thinking that she had truly lapsed into one of those mysterious cataleptic seizures. I then went up to her bedside, pulled the blanket back, and checked her pulse. There was nothing. What a stroke of unbelievable luck to realize that Dolores might be "alive but dead." I thought back to the words of Dr. Reynolds of Cambridge University. "The limbs can be readily moved by the observer, but they return to their former positions where they remain for hours or even days."

This prompted me to take Dolores by the wrist of her right arm and bring it upwards about two or three inches and then release it. Sure enough, her arm returned to its former position and just laid there like a lump of dead tissue. There was only one feasible way to tell if Dolores was experiencing a cataleptic condition. I would have to sit quietly by her bedside for at least the remainder of the day to see if she moved or awoke from her slumbers. And that's exactly what I did by placing myself in that big stuffed chair and watching the clock on her nightstand for the next twenty-four hours.

Ten-fifteen A.M. Bleary-eyed and hardly able to stay upright in my chair. As far as I could tell, Dolores had never moved an inch over the last twenty-four hours. Nothing it seemed had been disturbed, not even the blue nightgown that she always wore to bed. But just to make certain that what I was experiencing was real, I climbed out of the chair, bent down until my mouth was less than six inches from her right ear, and screamed DOLORES! No movement, not even a twitch. It seemed impossible and a bit too convenient, but it appeared that she was in a deep cataleptic trance in which she appeared to be stone dead. Exactly how much longer she would remain in this state was unknown.

There was only one thing left to do, but I would have to summon up all the courage I possessed, much like crawling on my belly in broad daylight and lobbing a hand grenade into a German bunker. I managed to forced myself to go downstairs and call the Bronx-Lebanon Hospital less than five minutes from my house in Riverdale. Although I can't recall exactly what I said once the receptionist answered my call, it went something like this:

"Hello? Is this the Bronx-Lebanon Hospital? I have an emergency. Please send an ambulance to 56431 Fremont Street. I think my wife is dead."

"Is she breathing?"

"I don't think so."

"An ambulance will arrive within a few minutes."

I hung up the phone and went to a latticed window that looked out on the street. One minute seemed like a century. A white ambulance pulled up in the driveway, and two men carrying a stretcher and some medical equipment hurried to the front door. Before they could knock, I opened the door and led them upstairs to Dolores' bedroom. As soon as we entered the room, one of the attendants ran up to her bedside and placed a stethoscope on her chest while taking her pulse. The expression on his face was a good indication that he could not detect a heartbeat. In an instant, the other attendant hooked Dolores up to some kind of breathing unit and switched it on. It ran for several minutes until the attendant shook his head, disconnected it, and looked at me with a tinge of pity on his face.

"Are you this woman's husband?" he asked.

"Yes," I replied, while attempting to appear concerned.

"I'm sorry, but your wife is dead."

And that was it. The attendants placed Dolores on the stretcher, covered her with a white sheet, strapped her down, and away she went into the waiting ambulance. Finally, after twenty five miserable years living with that fucking cunt bitch, I was rid of her forever. Call it selfish if you want, but I found great satisfaction and self-fulfillment knowing that she was headed for one of those freezer compartments at the hospital morgue where she would remain until I decided what to do next. I also grew quite excited knowing that her body temperature while lying in that freezer at the morgue would drop far below normal rather quickly, thus eliminating the chance that she might wake up while inside the freezer. But even if she did, no one would be there to hear her pitiful screams of despair.

To make things look as normal as possible, I gave one of the attendants all the necessary information concerning the "deceased," such as her name, birthdate, place of birth, height, weight, eye color, hair color, Social Security number, and any known diseases that affected her. I believe I did say something about her neurotic tendencies and that she might have suffered a heart attack in her sleep. I also couldn't resist the temptation to pile on lie after lie about that cunt bitch, such as how heart failure runs in her fucked-up family, and how often she complained about not feeling well and experiencing dizziness and shortness of breath, two of the cardinal signs of an impending heart attack. My fabrications about the bitch appeared to have worked exceptionally well because the attendants nodded their heads in agreement and revealed that many of their emergency patients over the age of fifty suffer from the same identical symptoms.

After the ambulance drove away, I called Mrs. Greenberg and told her that Dolores had died from unknown causes. She could hardly say anything on the phone and just mumbled a few words. The receiver must've slipped from her hand because I heard a dull thud only moments later. Then I heard another sound but more like someone tripping over a piece of furniture. It was undoubtedly Mrs. Greenberg fainting or hopefully having a heart attack. She was never much good to me anyways, and after all, it was Mrs. Greenberg who introduced me to that cunt bitch in the first place. Whatever it might have been, I never heard another word from her which didn't bother me in the least. Strange as it may seem, I later learned that Mrs. Greenberg did indeed experience a myocardial infarction while on the phone and that she was dead before hitting the floor, at least according to one of her tenants living in the apartment directly across the hall. I didn't even bother to send flowers or attend her crummy funeral.

To help celebrate what had occurred, I went downstairs, placed an LP of Chopin's preludes on the turntable, turned on the Marantz amplifier, rolled the volume control to eight, and stood in rapture as the Klipsch speakers filled the basement with sonic bliss. To make the moment even more enjoyable, I went back upstairs and started playing the Pleyel piano along with the LP spinning in the basement. The sound was overwhelming, and for the first time in many years, I truly enjoyed the music of Chopin without that cunt bitch hovering over me like a ravenous hyena. For some unexplainable reason, my hands glided over the keyboard with far greater accuracy than at any time in my life as a musician. My elation was so great that I stripped off my clothes and sat ass naked on the piano bench, laughing like a madman in a straightjacket while enjoying the cool, spring-like wind tickling the hairs on my sagging ball sack.

About an hour later and after putting my clothes back on, the hospital coroner called and asked what my plans were regarding Dolores' funeral and if she had any life insurance. At this point, I simply didn't give a shit and told the coroner that Dolores had always insisted on cremation and wanted her ashes to be given to Mrs. Greenberg. But of course, this was now impossible, so I told the authorities to do whatever they thought was best under the circumstances. After the coroner hung up, I removed my clothes again and played the Pleyel piano for the remainder of the day. By eleven P.M. that evening, total exhaustion had taken over, so I put my clothes back on and went to bed. I slept for two whole days without dreaming or even thinking about that bitch who by this time was screaming in Hell as Satan fucked her in the ass with a red-hot iron dildo.

Early the next morning, feeling totally refreshed and clear headed, I called up an old friend of mine in Paris who was once the lover of my late great aunt Matilda sometime prior to the outbreak of the Great War, circa 1913. Although I had known Pierre Lamontaigne since I was a child, I didn't actually know that much about him except that he was one of France's greatest living Abstract-Expressionist painters and had known Pablo Picasso intimately as comrades in the arts. As an indication of his talent, some of his paintings could be found hanging on the walls of the prestigious Louvre museum.

With that cunt bitch Dolores out of my life, I could now proceed with my plans. First of all, I purchased an expensive security system and had it installed in my house in Riverdale. I then locked up the house and made certain that everything was covered over, especially the Pleyel piano, the bronze bust of Chopin, and all of the windows that looked out on the street. After making sure that everything was safe and secure, I called Pierre again and asked him if he could find suitable but temporary lodgings for me in the city of Paris. I say temporary because the focal point of this plan was to purchase an estate known as Chateau d'Herouville where

Chopin lived for a short period of time during his tenure with George Sand. This chateau is also allegedly haunted by the ghost of Chopin. Built sometime around 1740, this mausoleum of death is located in the Val d'Oise region about thirty-five miles outside of Paris, and after making a few inquiries, I was told that the chateau was in need of some extensive renovations. But thanks to my late aunt Matilda and some investments I had made without Dolores' knowledge, I had plenty of cash to spend on this chateau in which I planned to live out my days after having all of my belonging shipped over from the States and then settle down to play my magnificent Pleyel piano in the spiritual shadow of the great Chopin.

But for some mysterious reason, I still wasn't convinced that Dolores was dead. The hospital attendants that came to the house said she was deceased, but I had my suspicions. A person can experience a cataleptic trance that lasts for hours or days and then all of a sudden, they wake up as if nothing has happened. However, if Dolores did wake up at the hospital or at the morgue before they slipped her in the freezer or performed an autopsy (imagine disemboweling a living body), it only makes sense that the authorities would have contacted me and said, "We made a horrible mistake. Your wife is alive, here at the hospital." But that didn't happen. Perhaps I've read too much of Edgar Poe, especially "Fall of the House of Usher" in which Roderick Usher buries his sister Madeline alive in her tomb, knowing all along that she's afflicted with catalepsy.

In order to set my mind at perfect ease, I drove down to the Bronx-Lebanon hospital to talk with the authorities. A nice-looking nurse with big tits led me down a set of stairs that opened up into a large room with an old gray-haired man in a white uniform sitting at a desk. Directly behind him and a bit above, a sign was engraved with the word MORGUE.

"Excuse me," I said to the old man. "I'm here to find out about my wife."

"What was your wife's name?"

"Dolores. Dolores Underwood."

"Oh, *that* one. Very strange, very strange, indeed."

"Wha…what do you mean, strange?"

"Are you her husband?"

"Yes."

"Well, after they brought her here, I slid her in the freezer. A few minutes later, there's some hard knocking on the freezer door. I opened it up and…"

"And what?"

"Well, there was nothing. She wasn't moving at all. I checked her pulse and everything and there was nothing. She was stone cold dead."

"Yes," I replied nervously, "that is very strange. Are you sure she's dead?"

"As dead as Hell."

"I see. Well, I'd like to have her cremated."

"You'll have to call the Bronx County Health Department." The old man flipped through a register of some kind and stopped after lighting one of those fucking filthy cigarettes.

"I see here that you've already requested cremation from the coroner."

"Yes, that's true."

"Then you don't have to do anything. They'll be here to pick her up in about twenty minutes. But I need you to sign some papers."

The old man reached in a drawer and placed several official-looking forms on the desk.

"You can fill these out here," he said, "or take them home and mail them back."

"I think I'll just take 'em home." Even though his cigarette smoke was burning my eyes, I thanked the old man for his courtesy, retrieved the forms, and started back up the stairs when the nurse with the big tits smiled at me.

"Is everything OK?" she asked.

"Yes, everything's fine, I replied while ogling those big tits. "Thank you for being so kind."

I then smiled back at her, all the while thinking how wonderful it would be to jamb my face between those luscious tits. By the time I reached the hospital parking lot and climbed in my car, a sensation of utter triumph overcame me, and I felt more alive than I had in many years, simply by knowing once and for all that the cunt whore Dolores was really dead and was by now stiffened like a length of salami in a walk-in freezer. Just before I pulled out of the hospital parking lot, I switched on the car radio and to my astonishment, my favorite station was playing Chopin's Prelude in D minor. This, I mumbled to myself, validated my actions and confirmed that my future life would be peacefully spent in the idyllic beauty of the Val d'Oise in north central France, the home of Chopin's Chateau d'Herouville. When I feel like this, I'm always reminded of what my good friend and confident Pierre Lamontaigne once said when I was a much younger man. "Murder," he related, "is the natural language of excited feeling. When a man is under the influence of this strongest of all emotions, his character becomes more elevated. Thus, he soon belongs to a higher order of imagination," something that is required for what many have called the "perfect murder."

Movement No. 3

Geographically, the region known as the Val d'Oise is not quite as attractive as other regions of France further to the south, due to being somewhat flat and geologically smooth which makes it very suitable for farming and vineyards. Yet is it renowned by all Frenchmen for its magnificent dark forests that form a sort of natural barrier to the north and south of the city of Paris. This geographical fact was discovered perhaps too late by those fucking stupid Nazis during the Second World War when they encountered a forest so thick that it was impossible to see more than ten feet distant. Many of the trees in this area include towering oaks, whitewashed birch, and juniper which together form a collection of foliage that is wonderful to behold in spring and autumn.

Many ancient trees dot the landscape, some as old as the 1428-1429 Siege of Orleans during the Hundred Year's War in which Jeanne d'Arc was victorious for France, the nation she so loved and adored that she voluntarily gave up her life by being burned alive at the stake. Not too distant from Chopin's "haunted house" lies the ancient city of Pontoise on the Oise River which boasts the smallest cathedral in France, built in the early thirteenth-century in the Gothic style. By sheer coincidence, one of my favorite French composers, Claude Debussy, was born in this area in Saint-Germain near the Oise River in 1862.

Several hours after locking up my house in Riverdale and throwing a few belongings and some clothes in a suitcase, I drove to LaGuardia Airport in Queens to board a plane (first class, of course) to the glittering city of Paris, the home of Notre Dame Cathedral and the Arc de Triomphe at the western end of the famous Champ-Elysees. I would like to mention that before leaving the house, I burned Dolores' diary in the fireplace as a sort of symbolic gesture of that cunt bitch being roasted to death at the crematorium. This final act also served as a kind of catharsis that allowed all of my hatred for that bitch to evaporate, never to trouble me again.

The flight from LaGuardia to the Paris North Airport was uneventful except for one incident that set into motion an entire sequence of weird and unexplainable events. While on the plane, I had the strangest feeling I was being watched, and I'm not referring to the stewardesses. The man sitting next to me in the window seat almost slept through the entire flight which took about seven hours, and during this time, I kept turning around in my seat, sensing that someone was watching my every move. Several times during the flight, I left my seat and wandered up and down the aisle, thinking that perhaps someone I knew was aboard the flight.

But I recognized no one; however, one of the stewardesses did resemble that cunt bitch Dolores, but I shrugged it off as a coincidence and returned to my seat. Yet during the whole time I was on the plane, I felt extremely uncomfortable, almost as if an unseen entity was standing in the aisle next to where I was sitting, gloating over me like Poe's imp of the perverse. When we landed in Paris, I remained seated until the plane was totally empty of passengers, yet still I felt the presence of something or someone lurking behind the seats or maybe in the back of the plane.

When I arrived at the apartment of my friend Pierre Lamontaigne, we had a long conversation on how difficult it was going to be to restore the Chateau d'Herouville to a livable condition, not to mention how much it was going to cost. According to Pierre whose knowledge on the chateau far exceeded my own (Pierre was also a well-known scholar on the life and times of Chopin), the estate was constructed sometime around the early 1740's by a Frenchman named Henri Gaudot who attended the famous Architectural School of Rome as a young man. Gaudot was so impressed by the surrounding landscape that he built his chateau directly on top of the remains of an earlier structure built in the middle years of the sixteenth century. It has been said that this earlier structure had been built directly over a graveyard dating back to the Crusades.

When Gaudot died in 1820, the chateau was utilized as a relay station for couriers traveling on horseback between the cities of Versailles and Beauvais. Allegedly, around 1875, Vincent Van Gogh was hired by the owners of the chateau to paint its exterior. Whether this is true or is nothing more than local folklore is not known. However, Van Gogh, along with his beloved brother Theo, is buried in the municipal cemetery of Auvers-sur-Oise, not too distant from the chateau. Pierre also related that the chateau was currently owned by a woman named Colette de Jouvenel, the daughter of the French novelist Sidonie-Gabrielle Colette who was nominated for the prestigious Nobel Prize in Literature in 1948. Strange enough, Madame Colette the novelist is buried at Pere-Lachaise Cemetery in Paris, the final resting place of Frederic Chopin.

Pierre and I also talked at length about that cunt bitch Dolores and how lucky I was to have discovered her weakness for catalepsy. His concerns over protecting me from the police greatly exceeded my expectations, for he made every effort to assure me that the cunt bitch would never bother me again. Interestingly, Pierre's own wife Ann-Marie had died under mysterious circumstances several years earlier, providing the Parisian police with good reason to suspect that Pierre was her murderer. "It's not every day," he said to me after throwing back a shot of expensive French brandy, "that someone falls from the third level of the Eiffel Tower after consuming a bowlful of orange sorbet ice cream." Of course, deep in my blackened heart, I knew that Pierre had killed his wife because much like that cunt bitch Dolores, Ann-Marie hated art and thought that her husband's paintings were nothing short of trash and belonged in a bonfire.

To my great delight and astonishment, Pierre requested that I spend some time at his apartment as his guest and also proofread the last chapter of his definitive biography on the life of Chopin which was to be published by a famous Parisian publishing house. With some trepidation, due to not being a true scholar, I agreed to proofread his work and settled down in bed at around eleven P.M. with the intention of reading the entire chapter in one evening.

As soon as I glanced at the first page of the chapter, I began to experience the same feeling that I had while aboard the flight to Paris, a weird feeling that someone was observing me from the shadows. I immediately climbed out of bed and went to a large bay window that provided an excellent view of the Eiffel Tower. In my warped mind, I imagined seeing Ann-Marie plummeting to her much-deserved death after being pushed by her husband from the third level of the tower. I slid open the window and glanced down on the street some four stories below. Not a single soul was in sight. After closing the window, I looked under the bed like a frightened child, then searched a clothes closet, finding nothing out of the ordinary except for a few dresses that once belonged to that other cunt bitch Ann-Marie. The bedroom door was firmly locked, so it would have been impossible for anyone to enter unseen. Like the experience aboard the plane, I shrugged off the feeling of being watched and went back to bed, where I started in on reading Pierre's final book chapter.

As I mentioned earlier, here on Death Row, prisoners are restricted to the type of reading material they can have in their cells. Out of all the things I could have with me to help pass the time (strange, to help pass the time to my own death), the only reading material I have at this moment is Pierre Lamontaigne's final book chapter for his biography on Chopin which unfortunately was never published because Pierre was shot to death about two weeks after I arrived at his apartment in Paris. Although I suspect that I know the identity of his killer, Pierre's death remains unsolved by the Paris police. With this in mind, I'll read the chapter to you because I'm convinced that Pierre knew that he was composing a premonition or foreshadowing device about his own death as well as my future life, part of which has obviously come true because here I am, sitting in my jail cell at Sing-Sing prison, waiting for my appointment with "Old Sparky:"

"CHAPTER NINE:
THE DEATH OF FREDERIC CHOPIN"

"By the time that Chopin had attained the age of thirty-seven, it had become quite evident to his friends and associates that he was destined for an early grave. In 1847, Chopin's physical condition had deteriorated significantly. His friend Monsieur Mathias remarked that observing Chopin in his deathbed was a "painful experience" and that it summoned up a "picture of total exhaustion. His back was severely bent, his head bowed as if strapped to a heavy weight;" however, he somehow managed to maintain an air of amiability. Another close friend provided a more detailed description of the dying composer: "Observing him so pale and thin, one would think that he had been dying for a long time, but then unexpectedly, he would cheer up and act as if nothing was the matter with him." Oddly, Chopin's health seemed to fluctuate and at times, he was able to walk unassisted down the boulevards of Paris. An instance of this fluctuation was recalled by one of Chopin's music publishers who stated that the composer told him "Perhaps I will get well again" which unfortunately was a cruel illusion.

By this time, Chopin was unable to accept pupils on a regular basis which negatively affected his main source of income. All of the money that he had been paid while touring Great Britain was gone and unknown to him, some of his closest friends had donated funds for his well-being, one being Madame Francesca Rubio who sent Chopin 25,000 francs. Whether the composer was fully aware of this generous gift is not clear, yet it appears that someone had intervened to make certain that Chopin's delicate pride had not been damaged. To make matters more disconcerting, Chopin's medical advisor, Dr. Michel Molin, suddenly died from an unknown ailment. According to Chopin, "I felt his loss keenly and was profoundly discouraged. No one could replace him, and I fell into a state of superstitious depression." However, Chopin eventually relented and allowed Dr. Anton Blache to replace the late Molin. "I'm quite certain," admitted Chopin, "that he will help me the most as a physician for children since, I must admit, there is still something of a child within me."

By early October of 1849, Chopin found it almost impossible to sit up in his bed without some kind of assistance, thus making it necessary for him to utilize hand gestures in order to make himself understood. For his own sake, Chopin was fortunate to have friends who loved him and were willing to care for his needs, such as his sister Ludwika Jendrzejewicz with her husband and daughter, and former pupil Adolphe Gutmann of whom Chopin stated was "dearer to himself than that of any other person." According to legend, it was Ludwika who, upon acting on her brother's instructions, had his heart removed from his body after death and preserved in a jar filled with some type of liquid (some say it was cognac), then placed inside of a mahogany casket that was smuggled out of France. Today, Chopin's heart lies in a reliquary at the Holy Cross Church in Warsaw, Poland.

As is the case with any number of famous personalities regardless of time and place, there are some mysterious circumstances related to Chopin's last days on earth that are, for the most part, completely devoid of hard supportive evidence. The most interesting of these circumstances is the alleged visit of George Sand to Chopin's sickroom at his apartment at 12 Place Vendome in the city of Paris. As noted by some sources, it seems that Sand sent an unknown lady to see Chopin; other sources declare that Sand herself showed up at the apartment but was turned away by Adolphe Guttmann, due to feeling that Sand's presence could "disastrously affect the patient" despite the fact that Chopin was already near death. Of course, there is the possibility that Gutmann's refusal was based on other reasons, one being that Sand was detested by many of Chopin's friends as a result of her reputation for being a lewd and lascivious woman. Another possible reason might have been based on the attitudes of some of Chopin's closest associates that Sand had ruined his life, that she was nothing more than a *manguese des hommes* or a "man-eater."

Following Chopin's death, the Reverend William Elliot Hadow who allegedly was present at Chopin's death-bed, wrote in his personal journal that Gutmann's decision to turn Sand away at the door was probably a good choice, even though Chopin had "spoken about her and wondered about her absence." However, Hadow observes that in most instances, the "fire of life is sacred at its lowest embers, thus a breath of love might have fanned (Chopin and Sand) into a purer flame" in which their past emotional attachments might have been rekindled, at least for a short period of time. Hadow adds that "In all of Chopin's story, there is nothing more pathetic than the narrow chasm which separated two severed hearts at the very point of reunion." Although academic speculation is often frowned upon, it is feasible that Chopin's passage into the unknown was made somewhat less difficult without the presence of George Sand.

Madame Elise Gavard, for whom Chopin wrote and dedicated Waltz in F minor, Op. 70, No. 2 in 1847, provides an excellent reminiscence on how Chopin was cared for during his last hours on earth. In my opinion, the first line of this remembrance conjures up the idea that Chopin may have died from congestive heart failure:

"In the back room of his apartment lay Chopin, tormented by fits of breathlessness and held up in his bed in the arms of his good friend Adolphe Gutmann. Seated near Gutmann was Princess Marcelina Czartoryska, a former piano pupil, who never left Chopin's side and nursed him like a sister of mercy without betraying her deep personal sorrow for her great mentor. Other friends provided Chopin with as much assistance as they possibly could, such as running errands to the doctor's office or the apothecary, and standing by the apartment door to prevent intruders from entering Chopin's apartment." The presence and contributions of Czartoryska cannot be overstated, for it has been reported that she spent many hours each and every day at Chopin's side, up until the very moment of his death.

Like most artistic individuals born and raised in the environment of Western and Central Europe during the early nineteenth century, Chopin exhibited a tendency for superstition which he allegedly gleaned from reading Slavonic poetry. In effect, this tendency impressed upon Chopin that his death was to be premature while remaining serene and acceptive. This attitude is more easily understood when we consider that "in several Slavic literatures, legions of shorter poems, embracing perfection in form, are seen as joys forever" and help to enrich the lives of their readers through particular revelations. However, these revelations are usually founded upon melancholy, one of the oldest Slavic characteristics, while pillared upon gloom, depression, and tragedy. Therefore, it is not surprising that Chopin admitted to one of his physicians that Slavic poetry "often provides a rare favor when it reveals the moment of the approach of death."

A rather commonplace result pertaining to the death of a famous artist like Chopin is the disregard of the artist's personal wishes by his alleged friends, associates, and in Chopin's case, his musical publishers. According to Auguste Franchomme, a well-known French cellist of whom Chopin greatly admired, it is a "pity that those who had the responsible guardianship of his manuscripts did not respect his dying desire," being that only his superior compositions were to be gifted to the public and that the remaining compositions be destroyed. However, this did not occur, for almost all of Chopin's musical compositions were later published, mostly by Pleyel, the manufacturer of Chopin's favorite piano. Thus, it is feasible that perhaps half of Chopin's Preludes might never have been published if Pleyel and other publishers had adhered to Chopin's final request concerning his music.

By the late second week of October, 1849, Chopin's health took a turn for the worse related to his ability to breath properly. Certainly, Chopin knew that he was on the verge of death which prompted him to call for a Polish Catholic clergyman to serve as a witness for the confession of his sins, something which he had not done for many years. On the 17th, Adolphe Gutmann allegedly helped Chopin to drink some red wine, whereby Chopin kissed Gutmann's hand and whispered "Cher ami" or "dear friend." These were Chopin's final words before "passing into the eternal silence" of death. The exact cause of his death has not been fully determined, but it is generally accepted among biographers and scholars alike that Chopin died from complications related to pulmonary tuberculosis. Some have suggested that he suffered from a then-unknown form of epilepsy.

Despite the fact that Chopin had been ill for quite some time, the music-loving people of France were shocked when news of his death began to circulate within the city and beyond. An unidentified reporter for the French newspaper *Le Correspondant*, a liberal Catholic publication, wrote that "Everyone who had come into contact with Chopin felt his death as a personal sorrow, whether being once honoured by his friendship, enriched by his musical genius, or gladdened by some kind word or pleasant greeting, even as a stranger. In effect, even a chance acquaintance with the master had given many a glimmer into greatness."

It would appear that Chopin's body had been placed in a rather decorative casket in the imposing Church of the Madeleine prior to his funeral. As Moritz Karasowski, author of *Frederic Chopin: His Life and Letters* relates, friends and admirers from all over Paris "came to look at the dead artist" who was surrounded by floral tributes which made Chopin appear to be "sleeping in a garden of roses amid which his face looked beautiful and young." Chopin's official funeral occurred on October 30th (appropriately Halloween Eve), and as noted in the prestigious periodical *Musical World* for November 10, 1849, the funereal scene was "one of the most imposing we ever remember to have witnessed. More than three thousand people assembled to take part in Chopin's burial rites."

Black curtains emblazoned with Chopin's name in silver were hung from the magnificent doors of the Church of the Madeleine and his coffin was carried by a list of notable pallbearers, including French painter Eugene Delacroix and piano manufacturer Ignace Pleyel, along the three-mile long boulevard from the church to the cemetery of Pere-Lachaise. According to some accounts, Chopin was buried in his evening clothes or concert dress, a long-held Polish custom in which the deceased is given the right to choose his burial clothes. Thus, in the end, it is only fitting that Frederic Chopin was interred not too distant from the awe-inspiring tomb of Abelard and Heloise, the infamous pair of lovers during the middle years of the tenth century C.E. Although their lives have been highly romanticized, with Heloise as a young French nun and Abelard as her older teacher, theologian, and seducer, their scandalous lover affair compares favorably with that of Chopin and George Sand, scandalous yet founded on a shared love for music and mischief."

Since I had only seen old daguerreotypes of the Chateau d'Herouville, some taken after Chopin's death, I made arrangements through a lawyer that represented the younger Colette to explore the estate and determine exactly what was required to bring it back to its former architectural beauty. When I informed the younger Colette of my intentions, she was overjoyed, due to her love for the estate and knowing that it would take a large amount of capital to restore it, capital that she did not have at her disposal. Upon arriving at the encrusted wrought-iron entry gate that stood some twelve feet high, I was let in by a groundskeeper who seemed to be totally ignorant as to why I was even there, but after I attempted to explain in poor French that Madame Colette had provided her permission to explore the estate, the groundskeeper opened the gate and told me in broken English that I would be sorry that he opened it. He then went about his business, disappearing around the corner of a small storage building that resembled a stone mausoleum with a *fleur-de-lis* motif set above the rusted iron door.

Architecturally, there are two sections to the chateau. First, there's the main three-story house with Gothic arched windows and an upper attic, much like a garret stylized with an old-fashioned mansard roof with a steep angle and punctured with dormer windows. The lesser section is two stories high and is attached to the main house by a double-story breezeway or short hallways. About thirty feet to the right of the main house is a similar structure that was probably used as guest quarters. The grounds are typical of the landscape in this part of France with a variety of trees and shrubbery. There was also what appeared to be an ancient swimming pool which I later learned was an eight-sided stone drinking trough designed for watering thirsty horses traveling between the village of Herouville, the city of Paris, and outlying provinces like Normandy (Rouen), Languedoc (Toulouse), and Champagne (Troyes).

Just as I had imagined, the interior of the main house was in utter shambles with interior sections of the walls totally collapsed. Large pieces of original plaster slats and debris were scattered haphazardly, making it somewhat treacherous to walk from one room to another, meaning that any holes in the floor were covered over, thus allowing the explorer to plummet to unknown regions beneath the chateau or through the floor of the second story. My first thought after seeing all of this destruction was wishing I could find the sons of bitches responsible for it and hang them up with barbed wire wrapped around their fucking balls.

The ceiling, once beautiful to behold with decorative cornices, heraldic medallions, fanciful moldings, and other plaster enrichments, had fallen into dire disrepair with numerous holes that allowed one to see the upper chambers from the ground floor level, sometimes even the sky itself. Many pieces of antique furniture like dining room chairs, divans, and tables, along with lamps and chandeleirs of Galle and Venetian, had been smashed without any concern for their value and beauty with the furniture broken up and used for kindling by trespassers and squatters over the decades. Of course, all of the window panes and delicate lattices had been broken out which made it possible for birds to make their nests in every nook and cranny throughout the chateau. In addition, all of the doors were either missing or had been stolen for their exquisite workmanship in oak or mahogany. Like I've already said, the people responsible for this destruction deserve nothing short of a horrible death, perhaps a good old-fashioned drowning in the stone drinking trough with a lead weight tied around their fucking necks.

After exploring a good portion of the chateau, I discovered an iron staircase spiraling upward into the darkness, and as I stood there, sunlight filled the area like a shaft of diffused gold at the bottom of a mineshaft. Since I had studied a set of blueprints provided by Madame Colette several weeks earlier, I knew that this staircase led up to the famous great room known colloquially as the George Sand Hall, referred by some architectural historians as the "Holy of Holies" located beneath the difficult to access attic of the south wing. According to my documentation, this is where Chopin installed one of his precious Pleyel pianos at the behest of his "girlfriend" Ms. Sand. Legend says that Chopin hired some stone masons from Paris to remove the northern second floor exterior wall of the chateau, install a set of pulleys and levers to raise the piano to the attic room which measures approximately forty feet wide, fifty feet deep, and about twelve feet in height, and then replace the exterior wall exactly as it had been before the demolition after the piano was safe and secure.

The acoustics, or so I've been led to believe, were superior, much like an auditorium specially designed for percussive stringed instruments like the piano. Technically, the room was designed in such a way as to favor the vibrations and resonances or modes of vibration that are created by the strings when in motion, known as sinusoidal sine waves. Chopin, being a purist, insisted that the piano soundboard must be of high impedance so that it vibrates vigorously. This insistence may have had something to do with the sound allegedly achieved by the great master in this "Holy of Holies" circa the mid 1840's with George Sand standing nearby or better yet, leaning on the piano with her cunt pushed up against the soundboard.

After climbing the staircase with some of its heavy iron bolts literally pulling themselves away from the brick mortar, creating a rather treacherous and wobbly climb, I reached the top floor which to my great surprise was still quite solid and free of debris. As I stood there, I imagined what this place must've been like almost a hundred and twenty years ago with Chopin seated at his Pleyel piano and composing new pieces of music as the vibrations from the plucked strings echoed haunting melodies that no living person had ever heard before, except for perhaps Ms. Sand who at the time was allegedly "shacking up" with Chopin at the chateau. Exactly how Chopin's Pleyel piano was removed from this room after his death is unknown, but some have suggested that it was pirated away piece by piece.

As I approached the middle of the room, I noticed an old dilapidated piano bench encrusted with sickening layers of ancient black paint and with one leg broken off at the tip. The original brass hinges were missing, so I removed the top of the bench and found a few shards of composition paper, the remnants of a quill pen, and a five-sided green glass inkwell that had long lost its contents. Were these objects once the property of the great master himself?

No sooner had I picked up the glass inkwell to examine what collectors call the pontil or the scar left over by the glassblower's blowpipe once it is snapped off from the base, I heard an odd noise, almost as if someone was humming from the depths of the wobbly wrought-iron staircase. Could it be Chopin's ghost, I wondered, or maybe Ms. Sand, wandering the dark corridors of the chateau in search of an orgasm? I would hope that Ms. Sand would employ some great delicacy in her pursuit of Chopin whose physical makeup at the age of thirty-five resembled a delicate, convoluted morning glory flower, a single trumpet suspended on a thin stem, and so gentle that the slightest disturbance would send it tumbling to the floor to wither away and die.

I then noticed that a small section in the corner of the attic wall had managed to pull itself away from the surrounding plaster. I instantly thought that more treasures like the quill pen and the glass inkwell might be concealed behind it. Fortunately, the attic room was well-lit and as I bent down, I could see something inside of the wall, so I reached in and found a small, leather-bound book with a gilt title. *A Collection of Slavic Poetry.* When I opened the book, I couldn't believe what I was fucking seeing, for written at the top of the second blank page was the name of the master himself. I was holding something that Chopin had most probably read late into the night while pondering his ever-approaching date with eternity and perhaps while George Sand frigged herself only a few feet from Chopin in the same bed.

Since I considered myself as a rather ardent scholar on the life of Chopin, I knew for some unrecognized reason that the national poetry of his native Poland had been grossly neglected. However, Poland's beautiful national dances, such as the pompous and graceful Polonaise, the bold Mazur (Mazurka), and many others, were still much admired by the Polish people who considered them as unique artistic treasures, a view also shared by Chopin who so wisely exploited them for his own musical pleasure.

As I've previously told you, the people in charge of this mausoleum called Sing-Sing prison will only allow an inmate on Death Row to have certain types of reading materials, thinking that the inmate could possibly invent some way of escaping through the help of an article published in a magazine like *Mechanics Illustrated.* For instance, "How to Make a Smoke Bomb with a Box of Strike Anywhere Matches." I think you get the basic idea. So, along with my late friend Pierre Lamontaigne's final book chapter for his biography on Frederic Chopin, I was lucky enough to convince the warden of this fucked-up place to let me keep Chopin's poetry book in my jail cell so I could read it late into the night, just like my great and fucked over Polish mentor. The first poem in this collection is called "The

Orphan's Lament," written around 1840 in which an unknown narrator regrets his lonely life and feels like an unloved orphan in an uncaring world. This perfectly describes Chopin; it also perfectly describes myself as a prisoner waiting for his appointment with "Old Sparky." So, without further ado, here's Chopin's poem:

THE ORPHAN'S LAMENT

Far more unhappy in the world am I,
Even in the meadow where birds doth fly.
Little birds, they flutter merrily to and fro,
Singing sweet carols upon the green bough.
I, alas, wander like the birds of the sky,
Desolate, alone, and waiting to die.
No one befriends me wherever I go,
And my heart beats with sorrow and great woe.
How I wish to cease the grief in my heart;
But with a smile, I know my time will come for relief.
And although misfortune has struck hard and fast,
I still long for my precious blessings to last.
So I ask, if all else in the world has been given enough,
Then why as an orphan must I do without?

After finding the book of poetry hidden behind the plaster wall, I sat down on the wobbly old piano bench and gazed forlornly through a huge latticed window with all the panes shattered and the once-ornate latticework broken and warped by years of exposure to the elements. But for some inexplicable reason, I began thinking about that cunt bitch Dolores and how she must've suffered when she was burned alive in the ovens of the crematorium. To be explicitly blunt, I cherished a feeling of perverse pleasure in knowing that she died horribly while the attendants at the crematorium sat back, smoking their fucking cigarettes and laughing when they slid a fat person into the incinerator and anxiously waited for the temperature to reach 1,200 degrees Fahrenheit. I could just hear them saying, "Four hundred pounds of fat is like burning seventeen gallons of kerosene." Odd to think that a "customer" goes from the frigid environment of cold storage to the blast furnace of Hell in a matter of minutes, at least on a busy afternoon. But for Dolores, she must've burned up rather quickly, considering that her fat fucking ass was equal to about three gallons of jellied kerosene.

I then heard someone apparently climbing up the wobbly wrought-iron staircase which brought a quick end to my fantasizing about that cunt bitch Dolores being roasted alive in the crematorium. At first, I thought it might be the groundskeeper, curious as to what a strange American was doing at the Chateau d'Herouville. But when I left the piano bench and stood in front of the latticed window, I could see the groundskeeper cleaning up some debris lying near the wrought iron gates. Obviously, it wasn't the groundskeeper slowly climbing the winding staircase, unless of course he could be in two places at the same time. Despite my natural tendency as a cautious person, I somehow managed to walk over to the edge of the staircase and glance downwards. What I saw was beyond belief. It was Frederic Chopin.

Although I was looking at him from a rather odd angle, I could tell that he was somewhat short in height, perhaps no more than five foot six inches with sandy brown hair that curled ever so slightly. He appeared to be about thirty years of age and immediately reminded me of Poe's "Master" of the House of Usher, with a "cadaverousness of complexion, very pallid" with a nose "of a delicate Hebrew model" and a "finely molded chin" with an "expansion above the regions of the temple." Overall, Chopin the man, as best as I can recall, possessed a "countenance not easily to be forgotten."

When he reached the top of the staircase, Chopin turned his head, smiled pleasantly, and simply stood there as if waiting for me to scream and jump to my death through the remains of the latticed window. Of course, I was completely dumbfounded, standing there in the presence of the greatest improvisational musician of all time, and totally unable to say anything to him that would make sense, especially since I knew that his ability to speak English was rather limited. To my utter surprise, Chopin never said a fucking word and simply took a seat at the wobbly piano bench. He seemed mystified by the absence of his precious Pleyel piano and obviously did not realize that he'd been dead for almost one hundred and twenty years.

I had no doubt at the time that I was gazing at the ghost of Chopin whose spirit had been wandering the desecrated halls of Chateau d'Herouville for a very long time, perhaps in search of Dolores' favorite French slut whose cunt had probably seen its share of circumcised cocks and other types of probes. I'm not certain who related this tidbit of information to me, but I remember being told that piano music could often be heard by the local inhabitants of the village some two miles away, drifting here and there through open windows and doorways, lingering in the shadows of bedroom corners, or echoing high above the rooftops.

Chopin was wearing a velvet waistcoat, a black jacket, and a pair of gray trousers that appeared to have been recently ironed. He also had a red cravat tied around his neck and was holding a walking stick that appeared to be made from mahogany with what I thought was adorned with the head of a wolf. He instantly reminded me of what his dear friend James Hopkins once said, that he was "something of a dandy who always wore patent leather boots and light kid gloves, and who was very particular about the cut and color of his clothes." Interesting to think that Chopin, due to his extraordinary talent, was generally accepted by his neighbors and acquaintances despite looking like a pimp; better that, I guess, than a male whore who goes to bed every night with beer stains on his pink pajamas.

One other thing about him that I noticed immediately was his aristocratic bearing which I'm certain contributed to his ability to walk into a room and become its master. Lastly, for a very odd moment, I sensed that he was somewhat effeminate. Now I'm not saying that he was gay (that would've been alright with me), but what I mean is that I could see him writing letters to both his male and female friends with the same language and expression. Chopin certainly wrote 'love letters' to that alleged slut George Sand and probably to a select audience of male admirers, placing much emphasis on lines like "You do not require my portrait because I'm always with you and I shall never forget the pleasantness of your face and demeanor" or maybe "I would give anything to embrace you once again before I leave this miserable world."

Chopin remained seated on the wobbly piano bench for about two or three minutes at the most, then stood up and brushed away a bit of stray dirt that had collected on his coat sleeve. After glancing around the room and looking directly at me as if looking into a full-length mirror, he straightened out his red cravat and made his way to the top of the stairwell that spiraled down to the first floor of the chateau. Within a few seconds, he had disappeared down the staircase and briefly afterwards, I heard what sounded like the gentle closing of a door, followed by a few soft piano notes that I recognized from Prelude, No. 24 in D minor. An overwhelming convection of emotion swept over my body and mind, a sort of velvety tenderness, a kind of sensual elegance, a type of soothing mysterious balm that made me feel wholly alive for the first time in many years. When I heard the final three bass notes, it was as if someone had dropped three lead weights from a great height, causing the entire chateau to vibrate in tune. No doubt, the villagers at Herouville heard it too, much like in the past when Chopin's ghost played a melancholy prelude that drifted with softness and quickly dissipated.

After my astounding experience with Chopin's ghost, I decided to leave well enough alone and abandon my plans to restore the chateau to its former glory. My main reason for this decision was because I felt somewhat compelled to leave Chopin to himself so he could wander about the chateau freely and without any interruptions from the living. When I informed Madame Collette of my decision, she became quite upset, but after I explained to her what had happened, she relented and accepted the situation. To my astonishment, this woman thought I was a very handsome man who deserved a true taste of French customs. So, within a few minutes after a short discussion, we ended up in her exquisite Rococo bed, where we fucked for hours until the sheets were drenched with sweat and a little bit of blood.

When I returned to the late Pierre's apartment, I contacted the landlord, a balding, gin-soaked son of a bitch, and paid him a year in advance so I could stay close to the chateau, and after mixing a pitcher of vodka martinis, I leaned back on an antique divan upholstered in light blue velvet and made the decision to pay a visit to the Pere Lachaise Cemetery, the most visited "City of the Dead" in the civilized world, located on the Boulevard de Menilmontant in Paris. This magnificent acropolis is the final resting place for many famous individuals like novelist Honore de Balzac; Jean-Francois Champollion who deciphered the hieroglyphs of the famous Rosetta Stone; Georges Cuvier, the founder of modern paleontology; the Romantic master painter Eugene Delacroix; Paul Dukas, composer of the *Sorcerer's Apprentice,* and of course, Frederic Chopin, minus his heart.

As I approached the magnificent bronze gates of the cemetery, towering some twelve feet high and covered with a beautiful green patina, a young French girl was standing there holding a bouquet of red roses in her left hand. This was nothing out of the ordinary because it was obvious that the roses were for someone buried behind the massive stone walls. She smiled delicately at me, almost as if recognizing who I was, or perhaps knowing why I was there. To say that I was struck with an odd feeling would be pretty close to the truth, especially when she came up to my side and placed her right hand in mine and said in broken English, "I have a little story to tell you if you are here to see Monsieur Chopin."

"Who…who the hell are you?" I replied, totally mystified by her startling statement.

"My name is Violette," she said. "Please, come with me."

Upon entering the magnificent bronze gates of Pere Lachaise Cemetery, Violette began to relate the following experience about one of the times when she visited the "City of the Dead" to pay her respects to Chopin, the "Poet of the Piano":

"Darkness rested on the tombs, the cypress trees, and the silent marble faces with cold eyes written with grief. Darkness crept upon the flowers in their beds and overshadowed the gardens growing wild upon the older tombstones. Darkness also rested on the most beautiful tomb in this sanctuary of death, an epic in stone consecrating the grave of Frederic Chopin. High above a massive marble block of gray, carved with a portrait of the great master, the Greek muse of music, Euterpe, kneels in a posture of utter sadness, weeping over a broken lyre, her head bowed in deathly silence. I looked long on this monument, and watched others leave behind bouquets of aromatic flowers, violets and primrose, in remembrance of Chopin's majestic genius."

"And then, as I was about to say my farewells, I glanced at the statue of Euterpe and saw that her head had lifted upwards. She was now looking directly at me, yet her eyes remained full of sadness. "Block of gray," I whispered to myself, "truly you are alive in the city of the dead."

"When did all of this happen?" I asked Violette as she extended her hand and touched the head of Euterpe that was now in its normal bowed position, eyes slanted downwards.

"Last year," she replied, "on April 30th, my birthday, in the late afternoon."

April 30th. The day that Adolf Hitler blew his fucking brains out with his Walther pistol while sitting on a small sofa with the crumpled body of Eva Braun next to him. After Violette had finished relating her weird experience, we found ourselves standing within several feet of Chopin's grave. On the right side of the monument, a set of stone steps allowed some access to the grave where one could place his hand on the monument. As I was about to do just that, I heard a sound that seemed to come from *inside* the monument, a sound reminiscent of deep moaning. Violette heard it too, and I could tell from the expression in her pale blue eyes that she was utterly terrified.

"There were times in the past," said Violette, trembling, "when I fled from this place as fast as my feet would carry me. Sometimes, it was the voices of the dead; other times, it was when I came upon an open grave with the blood-red earth piled in heaps, and the spade of the gravedigger carelessly tossed to one side."

A single dense cloud slipped across the sun and threw deepening shadows on the marble gray tomb of Chopin. And then I heard the sound again, the sound of deep moaning, but this time, it seemed to be coming from somewhere higher up the stone steps, enveloped in a wall of blackness. For a fleeting moment, my mind turned to that cunt bitch Dolores whose fat ass was equivalent to about three gallons of jellied gasoline as she burned up in the crematorium. The young French girl looked at me rather oddly, giggled a bit and ran off down the boulevard until she disappeared into a thick blanket of fog. Mingling with the darkness, the song of a single nightingale echoed among the stones and I was quickly reminded of Samuel Taylor Coleridge's 1798 poem "The Nightingale: A Conversation Poem," especially the opening lines which for the first time in my miserable life brought about a sense of wrongful mischief for murdering poor Dolores:

> Most musical, most melancholy bird!
> In nature, there is nothing as melancholy,
> And for a night-wandering man whose heart is pierced
> With the remembrance of a grievous wrong,
> It is a song of neglected love, of unforgiven hate.

Was I feeling sorry for myself for killing that cunt bitch Dolores? Absolutely fucking not. All I had to do was think of how much she hated Chopin and how much she despised his music and his great musical gift to the world. I have always been convinced and still am that Dolores got what she deserved. In fact, she deserved it more than Pierre Lamontaigne's wife whom I know for a fact was pushed from the third level of the Eiffel Tower by her husband after consuming a bowl of orange sherbet (or sorbet) ice cream. She was pushed because she too was a cunt bitch, but not as bad as Dolores. Strange to think that Pierre's favorite film was *Vertigo*, Alfred Hitchcock's masterpiece of suspense and terror. Incidentally, Pierre's wife, Ann-Marie, bore a striking resemblance to Kim Novak, built like a brick shithouse with tits like torpedoes. I can only imagine what the stunned Parisians must've said when Marie's body hit the pavement, splattering about like a big scoop of red wine sorbet ice cream.

Emboldened by the need to know the source of the moaning, I slowly climbed the steps besides Chopin's tomb and discovered nothing out of the ordinary. Perhaps, I thought, it was a child playing a sick joke on a stranger, or it was merely a person whispering to someone else not too far away, drifting in the air like the scent of a funeral wreath intertwined with roses, violets, and carnations. Of course, the idea did cross my mind that it was that cunt bitch Dolores, that she had awaken from her cataleptic slumber just in time to save her fat ass from the bonfires of the crematorium and was stalking me like a Mohican Indian, skulking behind the trees and waiting for the right moment to jump out and plunge a knife in my back. Have I told you that Dolores was also a very sneaky bitch? It would not surprise me to know that she had managed to save enough of my money to follow me to Paris and haunt my ass like some disembodied cunt bitch ghost.

Even though I wanted to remain at Chopin's grave all fucking night and drink myself into a stupor with a fifth of French brandy I had brought along, I left the cemetery, still thinking about Violette and her strange encounter and that cunt bitch Dolores who might have escaped the inferno at the crematorium which if true would mean that the authorities were probably not far behind me. I then decided to pay a visit to the Louvre so I could see for myself some of Pierre Lamontaigne's abstract expressionist paintings that occupy this incredible building, along with masterpieces by Jacque-Louis David (1748-1825), Rembrandt Van Rijn (1606-1669), and Eugene Delacroix (1798-1863) who once stated that when he was sitting near a window that opened into a garden, presumably at Chopin's apartment in Paris, his piano music would drift through the airy currents, mingled with the sweet songs of nightingales and the aroma of roses in full spring bloom.

At the museum, and to my great disappointment, I could only locate one of Pierre's paintings on public display, along with some works by both French and American abstract expressionists. I was struck with awe by Pierre's painting entitled *Nude Descending into Hell*, his "homage" to the great Marcel Duchamp's *Nude Descending a Staircase* (1912) which I always viewed as an abstract woman in a shifting rhythmic poise merging into itself. It is much like the frames in a length of movie film that is moving through a projector extremely fast (100+ frames per second) in which the image is shifting under a powerful strobe light. Poor Pierre! Shot to death by an unknown motherfucker (I'm positive it was that cunt bitch Dolores) and unable to enjoy the prestige of having one of his works in the world-famous Louvre. I sincerely doubt that the curators and administrators of this place knew or even suspected that one of their artists was a cold-blooded, murdering monster with a liking for sherbet ice cream.

In my estimation, just because Pierre Lamontaigne was a murderer does not necessarily exclude him from the praise that he deserves as a serious and important artist, much like Chopin, considered by some of his contemporaries and biographers as a "pantywaist" (to quote that cunt bitch Dolores) and as a man who saw beauty in ugliness in relation to George Sand. In many respects, the artist should be regarded by society as a true anti-hero. What I mean by this is that the artist simultaneously exhibits good qualities (such as myself) and bad qualities, especially through a hatred for the establishment and the status quo.

In other words, he is the ultimate non-conformist, a social role in which I heartily place myself without reservation. A powerful example of this non-conformist attitude, as in the case of Pierre Lamontaigne, and others like him, is their position as bona fide members of the art movement known as Abstract Expressionism with some of its greatest adherents being Willem de Kooning, Jackson "Jack the Dripper" Pollock who died in an alcohol-related car accident in 1956, Franz Kline, and Robert Motherwell. Some have made the wild yet sensible observation that Abstract Expressionists like the late Pierre Lamontaigne created through their artistic output a serious threat to the human race, an indication that their art was so disturbing that it warped the minds of its viewers, setting into motion a sort of mental abstraction that turned some into full-blown anarchists and madmen.

Others have made the suggestion that Abstract Expressionism, especially works like Duchamp's *Nude Descending a Staircase,* served as the impetus to become an alienist or a person that intentionally separates himself from the rest of secular society, sometimes perhaps even the Universe itself. For myself, the words of Robert Motherwell sum up the entire arena quite nicely: "Abstract Expressionism creates the need for felt experiences, such as intense mental stimulation, immediacy, directness of action, a unified field, warmth, vividness" and of course, rhythmic pleasure as in Chopin's piano works. Was Chopin a musical Abstract Expressionist? I dare say, yes, indeed. These traits also apply to murder, specifically the warmth that fills the soul once the act is accomplished.

I might as well admit something to you that has plagued my mind for quite a long time. Am I going to Hell for murdering Dolores? If I do go to Hell, will she be there to fuck me in the ass with a red-hot dildo for eternity? While this totally abstract thought was floating around in my brain, I happened upon a particular painting at the museum by Eugene Delacroix entitled *Dante and Virgil in Hell,* otherwise known as *Barque of Dante,* first exhibited at the Exposition Universelle in Paris in 1855. The foundation for this work, a sort of shift from the neo-classical style to the Romantic, is that of a narrative painting or one that relates a story through its imagery. In this instance, the painting makes Virgil, the ancient Roman poet and author of the epic *Aeneid,* the honorary guide that leads Dante Alighieri, author of the *Divine Comedy* and *Paradise Lost,* through the bowels of Hell and Purgatory until reaching the Gates of Paradise.

For some mysterious reason, I was drawn to this painting as if the spirit of Dante himself had reached out from the grip of death to clasp what remained of my mortal soul. My first impression related to this strange occurrence was based on the motif of *Dante and Virgil in Hell,* being the sixth deadly sin or evil thoughts concerning Wrath or intense anger. As I have stated before, my anger against that cunt bitch Dolores was so overwhelming that I considered it my bound duty to kill her and send her soul into the Invisible. As Dante once remarked, it is always better to reign in Hell than serve in Heaven under the domain of a jealous and spiteful God. Of course, Dolores' absolute hatred for Chopin and George Sand was the driving mechanism for this intense wrath, similar to that of a madman like Albert Fish whose hatred for the human race propelled him to murder innocent little boys and store their shriveled-up penises in his refrigerator for later consumption at his ghastly dinner table.

I'm sad to report that my good friend in crime Maxie Sullivan was electrocuted last night shortly after twelve P.M. He walked the last few steps to "Old Sparky" like a real man without a single complaint. He also did it all by himself, telling the prison warden that he didn't need spiritual comfort from a non-existent God. That's what he told me weeks ago and he stuck to his word. Even though Maxie was responsible for the deaths of many individuals, most of whom deserved to be killed, he remains as my hero, a man of his word, who went to his death firmly defiant against society, a true non-conformist son of a bitch. In less than two days from this moment, I'll be joining Maxie in death via a short visit with "Old Sparky." I'm sure you must be wondering how I ended up here in Sing-Sing prison. Obviously, for you readers that just don't have any fucking intelligence, I obviously got caught related to murdering that cunt bitch Dolores, but not in the way you might suspect. So, with this in mind, I'll finish up my weird tale before my cell door grates open for my appointment with death.

Movement No. 4

On a fucked-up rainy afternoon when I wasn't feeling all that well, the balding, gin-soaked landlord of Pierre's apartment building showed up at the door unannounced while in the company of a strange-looking woman that bore a weird resemblance to Mrs. Greenburg, Dolores' aunt. All she said in rather poor English was that I had to vacate Pierre's apartment, even after I told her that I had paid the rent a year in advance. She was adamant and refused to consider a number of logical options I had in mind about staying in the apartment. But after giving it some thought, I decided to get the fuck out of the apartment and let the old French bitch have her way. After throwing some clothes in a gray suitcase and stealing a few items that once belonged to Pierre, such as a small bronze statue of Rodin's "The Kiss," I left the apartment and headed down the hallway. In many ways, I was glad to get the fuck out of there and return to New York before I became caught up with all the bullshit concerning Pierre and his cunt wife.

As I was about to leave the building, the old French woman (whom I assumed was the apartment building's owner) told me that the police had finally discovered that Pierre Lamontaigne, the Abstract Expressionist and non-conformist, had murdered his wife by pushing her from the third level of the Eiffel Tower. Thus, she wanted nothing to do with him, and as far as she was concerned, all of his belongings would be tossed in the garbage. With this, I asked her if I could take Pierre's things with me, whereby she smiled wryly and told me in broken English to fuck off and get the hell out of Paris.

And that's exactly what I did. I got the fuck out of Paris and headed for one last time to the Chateau d'Herouville, where the groundskeeper was busy raking up some debris around the house. He recognized me instantly and made some kind of a gesture with his right hand which I interpreted as meaning to get the fuck out of his life. Once again, that's exactly what I did. I then headed for the ancient city of Pontoise on the Oise River where I had spent some time at a run-down hotel making plans for the restoration of the chateau. After having a few vodka martinis at a quaint tavern on the Oise River, I called for a taxi, and as it drove away, I stared longingly through the rear window, watching the old and crooked lanes of the city disappear, along with the ramparts of ancient fortifications left over from the Battle of Orleans.

To be totally honest about it, I was deeply saddened to realize that these remnants of antiquity that had managed to survive the ravages of time and the onslaught of modernization would soon vanish forever. But at the same time, I felt a surge of confidence in knowing that Dolores had not survived the ravages of the crematorium. In fact, I was so confident that I made it my first priority once I returned to New York City to discover the truth about that cunt bitch.

Once I had boarded the plane back to New York City, it happened again, that weird feeling that someone was watching me, perhaps someone crouched down in a seat way in the back of the plane and playing a sick game of hide and seek. One of the stewardesses, a pretty blonde with shiny green eyes, noticed that I was feeling uncomfortable and asked if I would like a sedative so I could sleep all the way to New York. After I told her that I hated pills, she smiled pleasantly and reassured me that our flight would be nothing out of the ordinary.

I took her at her word, even though that weird feeling of being watched kept gnawing at me like the sense of impending doom. You might think I'm totally fucking crazy, but I swear that I heard someone call my name, just a whisper at first, then a bit louder. I turned in my seat and looked carefully at everyone sitting behind me. Most of them were sound asleep with a few reading books or magazines. The pretty stewardess with the shiny green eyes was busy making coffee and was softly talking to another stewardess about how much she missed being in New York City and getting fucked hard by her boyfriend. After turning back around in my seat, I thought about the voice that I heard at Chopin's tomb. It sounded like the same voice, but this was not possible. Finally, I relented and convinced myself that it was all in my head.

Upon my arrival in New York City, I became extremely paranoid thinking that Dolores was still alive. So to set my mind at ease, I returned to the Bronx-Lebanon hospital just to make certain that Dolores had met her end in the crematorium. At about two o'clock in the afternoon, I found myself heading down the same set of stairs at the hospital that led to the morgue where the same old gray-haired man in the white uniform was seated at a desk while filling out some forms.

"Excuse me," I said. "Do you remember me?"

The old man looked up from the desk and smiled broadly.

"Oh, yeah. I remember you. Can I help you with something?"

"Well, this may seem like a very strange request, but I need some information about my wife."

"Your wife?"

"Yes. Dolores Underwood."

"Oh, *that* one. Let me check my files."

The old man got up from the desk, slid open a dingy gray filing cabinet, searched through some manila folders, then removed one with a little note paperclipped to it.

"Oh, yes," said the old man after reading the note. "A very strange case here. Didn't you come here one time asking about your wife's cremation?"

"Yes, I did."

"According to the note, it seems there was some confusion about your wife being dead."

"Well, was she dead or not?"

"Of course, she was dead. I don't make it a practice to cremate living people. That would be cold-blooded murder."

"So, I guess she really was dead."

The old man stared at me with a puzzled look on his face. "Why do you think your wife was alive?"

"Oh, I'm just being stupid, I guess. This whole thing about my wife dying suddenly has really upset me. I just had to make sure she was dead."

The old man returned the manila folder to the filing cabinet, sat back down at the desk, and lit a cigarette.

"Listen, Mister Underwood," he said, after taking a long drag on the cigarette. "I've worked here for thirty years, and I've never cremated anyone that wasn't dead. Take my word for it. Your wife was dead as hell. If you don't believe me, then go to the coroner's office and check the cremation report."

"I don't think that's necessary," I replied, after wiping away some sweat with a handkerchief. "Poor Dolores. I hope she's in a better place."

The old man took another long drag on his cigarette, leaned back in his chair, and grinned like Frank Gorshin impersonating actor Burt Lancaster.

"Wouldn't that be something?" he said. "Burning someone alive. The police would have a fuckin' field day with that one. But since I just work here, it wouldn't be my fault unless the person woke up or moved."

He then turned his head and looked directly at me. "Nice job, Mr. Underwood," he said, sounding exactly like Burt Lancaster.

Shaken to the core of my soul would hardly explain how I felt at that moment. Did the old man know that Dolores had been burned alive in the crematorium? If he did, then why not just call the police and put an end to it? The old man was obviously Satan in disguise, gloating over his knowledge that I had committed one of the "Deadly Sins" with retribution being a stroll through the fire and brimstone of Hades.

A few minutes later, I was walking down the street outside the Bronx-Lebanon Hospital, thinking about that cunt bitch Dolores when a young woman sashayed down the sidewalk with her tits swaying back and forth like two cantaloupes in a gunny sack. As I made my way down the sidewalk, I came across the open doorway of an old sandstone-faced lecture hall, and next to the doorway, a standing sign proclaimed:

THE ORATORIO SOCIETY OF NEW YORK
PRESENTS RENOWNED MUSICOLOGIST
VIKTOR PADEREWSKI.
AN APPRECIATION OF FREDERICK CHOPIN

I could hear the voices of people coming from inside the lecture hall, along with a piano playing Chopin's famous Nocturnes, Op. 9, composed of three separate pieces dedicated to Madame Marie Pleyel, the daughter-in-law of Ignaz Pleyel, the founder of the piano company. Of course, I hurried inside and took a seat in the front row after paying three dollars to a gaunt-looking man who bore a shuddering resemblance to the late Pierre Lamontaigne. Moments later, a man dressed entirely in black with a red scarf tied loosely around his neck moved behind an old lectern and slowly scanned his sparse audience.

Don't fucking ask me why the warden of this fucked-up prison let me keep a copy of the lecture by Mr. Paderewski. Maybe he feels sorry for me, or he's in league with that fucking old man at the crematorium that talks like Burt Lancaster. Anyways, while sitting here in my dingy death-row cell and knowing that poor Maxie Sullivan's body is rotting away in an unmarked grave, I often read Paderewski's lecture late into the night when my heart is overjoyed with knowing that the ashes of that cunt bitch Dolores have by now been scattered to the wind and the waves of the filthy East River.

"AN APPRECIATION OF FREDERICK CHOPIN"

"First of all, I would like to point out that the compositions of Frederick Chopin are perhaps the most placid and harmonious of all the music created in Europe during the first half of the nineteenth century. If you disagree with this statement, may the Gods toss thee asunder into a pit of burning Hell. This remarkable tone poet was born near the beautiful city of Warsaw in 1810. His father was a Frenchman who according to legend was a decent painter of Polish landscapes, while his mother was a mere waif of a girl amid the verdant hills of her native Poland. When Chopin was about nine years of age, he made his first public appearance as a musical prodigy with extraordinary promise. It has been said that one of his earliest piano teachers was a man of somewhat equal talent who was implicated in the murder of a young village woman with few redeeming qualities. In 1828, Chopin departed from his native Poland with his sights set on the lavish city of Paris which at the time was experiencing a cultural renaissance. According to a popular Parisian journalist, writing sometime after the composer's death, Chopin "was a comet in the musical cosmos that soon vanished but not until leaving behind an immense impression on his era and the whole existence of musical history."

One of the first great European musicians to recognize Chopin's genius was none other than Robert Schumann, another piano virtuoso who attempted suicide in 1854 and was later diagnosed as suffering from acute psychotic melancholia and possibly other forms of neuroses. Several of Chopin's most famous piano works, such as *Variations on Don Giovanni,* Op. 2, written when Chopin was seventeen years old, revealed to Schumann through his keen vision the unmistakable genius of its young composer. During this period of time, circa 1827, Chopin was considered by many Parisians as an undoubtable master of the pianoforte, especially related to his *Concertos in E minor* and *F minor,* both of which assisted in opening the portal to a second career as a highly in-demand teacher.

With the city of Paris as his official base of operations, Chopin was welcomed and idolized as one of the great virtuosos, akin to painter Eugene Delacroix whose desire to be surrounded by beautiful music was a well-known fact in Paris. As Delacroix once remarked, "Nothing in this life can be compared with the emotions that arise from music which often creates within my mind states of exaltation, particularly the melancholy renditions of Monsieur Chopin. It is while under the spell of Chopin that I create some of my most beautiful and powerful paintings."

Like other artists whose lives parallel a precipice that steps off into the very bowels of the earth, Chopin was a sensitive individual in relation to his physical well-being. In his case, it was an undermining pulmonary disorder (some allude to tuberculosis or congestive heart failure) that hastened his death at the tender age of thirty-nine. Thus, in order to help alleviate his deteriorating health, Chopin visited the Spanish domain island of Majorca in the Mediterranean while accompanied by author Madame George Sand who was romantically bound to the great composer. The relationship between these two individuals has often been described as fiery as well as icy cold; however, it is clear from the surviving documentation that Chopin and Sand were intimate friends and lovers with Sand considered by some of Chopin's associates as being more of an emotional burden than a benefit. As Chopin's health continued to deteriorate, his relationship with Madame Sand also disintegrated, yet Chopin somehow managed to visit England and Scotland as a solo performer. After returning to Paris in October of 1849, Chopin died, thus depriving the world of one of its greatest and most influential musical geniuses of the nineteenth century.

Although the musical catalog of Chopin is currently confined to compositions for the piano, it is highly probable that he was also blessed with the ability to play other types of instruments that were popular during his lifetime, such as the guitar and the harpsichord. And much like Schumann, Chopin did not allow the technical rules and paradigms of accepted musical form to cloud his imagination. However, it would be ridiculous to say that Chopin's piano compositions are not without proper and more than adequate structural fundamentals. It would also be inappropriate to suggest that his musical tone poems, highly inspired by the Slavic poetry of his native Poland, are not superb examples of musical continuity related to harmony and coloration, thus rendering them as faultless and occupying the same musical spheres as that of Beethoven and Mozart. In addition, it is clear that Chopin was far more than merely successful in relation to his musical ideas and motifs which beyond any doubt are singularly poetic as tonal masterpieces.

If we look closely at Chopin's piano compositions, it becomes obvious that he depended a great deal upon his intuition and imagination as opposed to utilizing mathematical calculations or the works of others as inspiration. His mastery of his musical material is nowhere more obvious than in how he dealt with tonal details. Thus, in this respect, Chopin discovered as well as developed new ways of playing the piano, all of which was highlighted by his technical skills, musical refinement, and mode of expression that has never been equaled.

At this point, it would be safe to say that Frederick Chopin was the originator of a particular style of pianoforte melody and of a playing technique that was unknown (or perhaps unrecognized) prior to his time on this planet. One particular musician that possibly foreshadowed the techniques of Chopin was Johann Hummel (1778-1837), an Austrian composer and virtuoso pianist whose influence also touched the musical boundaries of Robert Schumann. Several scholars have maintained that Hummel's *Piano Concerto in B minor* can be perceived in a number of Chopin's own concertos. However, we can say with great certainty that Chopin's utilization of melody and harmony was utterly unique. Personally, I never tire of his vivid tonal images that reflect a realm of beauty that constantly brings tranquility and peace of mind.

In summation, in my humble opinion, any person that truly appreciates the music and artistry of Frederick Chopin is without doubt an exceptional human being. This is especially true if this person happens to consider himself as a musician and lover of everything that is good in this life and beyond it. If Chopin were alive today, he would surely grasp the hand of this particular person and express a sad lament for not having the time to know him better as a friend and confidant."

The last paragraph of Mr. Paderewski's lecture brings tears to my eyes every fucking time I read it. I should also mention that at the end of Paderewski's lecture, the musician at the piano began to play Chopin's highly recognizable Piano Sonata No. 2 in B-flat minor, Op. 35 with the third movement of this piece being the famous "Funeral March" or dirge that was composed about two years prior to the first, second, and third movements. At the beginning, I thought it was quite an appropriate way to conclude the lecture, but after leaving the lecture hall with the dirge echoing into the street, an extremely uncanny feeling came over me, much like something one might experience at a funeral for a dear friend, thinking that the next funeral he attends will be his own.

And then something really fucking weird occurred. Although it was broad daylight, it suddenly grew gray and ominous with a dark cloud obscuring the afternoon sun. The cloud partially dissipated, causing angular shadows and distortions in the buildings that reminded me of *The Cabinet of Dr. Caligari*, a German Expressionistic film made in 1920 that emphasized the application of light and shadow in order to generate an atmosphere of chaos and pandemonium.

Then I glanced across the street, and standing in the shadowed doorway of a business that sold Steinway pianos was that cunt bitch Dolores, totally naked and without any indication of having been burned alive. At that moment, I began to feel just like Cesare (Conrad Veidt), the walking dead somnambulist in *Caligari*. I could not move, and my breathing became shallow and strained. My arms and legs felt like rolled lumps of clay, and my heartbeat turned shallow and imperceptible. Sensing my reaction to her presence, Dolores exuded a gentle smile, laughed a bit and strolled away down the street with her ass jiggling like four gallons of jellied gasoline. I stumbled back inside the lecture hall where the unknown pianist, still seated at the piano, suddenly started playing Chopin's Prelude in D minor. When he finished playing the final three notes, he turned on the bench and looked straight at me. It was Frederick Chopin, ghastly beyond description with a gaping hole in his chest filled with maggots.

For some time now, I've been quite conscious of the fact that I'm on the verge of a nervous breakdown. While confined in this fucked-up jail cell, I've fought long and hard against this happening, but the pains in my head increase every single day and grow more acute with each passing hour. Old Maxie Sullivan is one lucky son of a bitch because he's dead and doesn't have to worry about all the shit that goes along with a visit with "Old Sparky." I also realize that the time is nearing rapidly when I will collapse entirely while confined in this fucked-up place and probably end up in a straightjacket. In many ways, it makes me feel glad to know that I won't be spending the rest of my miserable life in this fucking hellhole. I know that killing that cunt whore Dolores was wrong, but I don't think I deserve to go on suffering as I have for many months. Oh, well, life's a bucket of shit with a barbed wire handle, so I'm gonna empty that bucket of shit right here on the jail cell floor and hope that the warden steps right in it.

Do you recall what I said about Sing-Sing prison at the beginning of my narrative? That the food is not too shabby, and that I get to take a hot shower twice a week with a change of clothes once a week? Well, my friends, it's all a big fat, fucking dirty, filthy heathen lie. Here's that shit in the bucket that I mentioned a few sentences earlier. There are more than two hundred jail cells that are flush with the outer prison wall which I believe is about twelve feet thick with interior iron bars running parallel and perpendicular, a sort of crosshatch that makes it impossible to penetrate. So, during the months of July and August, moisture clings to the walls like slimy paste. My cell just happens to be one of these fucked-up holes. Most of these cells are occupied by two inmates instead of one for which they were initially designed, but the prison officials don't give a fuck who an inmate shares a cell with, meaning that someone imprisoned for simple assault might be sleeping with a convicted murderer, like myself.

Also, all of the jail cells in this shithole are infested with huge gray rats that like to nibble on fingers and toes that happen to stick out from under the blanket.

Speedy punishment by being flogged with a length of garden hose is normal around here, especially if a man attempts to ask for more food in the mess hall which is not clean nor sanitized to any degree. Maggots are everywhere. I've found them in my food and wriggling around on the tabletops. As to solitary confinement, located in the depths of the prison like some fucking dungeon at the Tower of London, it is pitch black, small, and filthy beyond description. You might not believe this, but some of the cells in solitary confinement have not seen the light of day in over eighty years. If a prisoner spends more than a day in these conditions (which is not at all unusual), he is forced to sleep in his own shit with a blanket that has been used to wipe an untold number of diseased fleshy assholes.

Since most of the inmates in this fucking place are in single jail cells, either three or four tiers above the red brick floor, when the guards decide to clean out the cells, they use a fire hose that allows the filth and grime to drip down from one tier to the next. This is especially vile when a cell high above has a broken toilet that won't flush properly. I think you get the idea here. Thus, life in these cells is pure torture, even for those who come from a segment of society that is accustomed to living in filth and decay. For myself as a sensitive and educated man, living day in and day out under these conditions brings a smile to my face, knowing that "Old Sparky" is waiting to relieve me of my suffering.

And here's the worst stench of that shit in the bucket. When I had somehow managed to find my way back to my house in Riverdale after Mr. Paderewski's lecture and seeing Chopin with his heart gouged out, I discovered that the front door was wide open. As soon as I walked in the house, I sensed that something was terribly wrong because small chips of black paint were scattered about on the living room carpet. When I swung open the door to the so-called "purple parlor," my eyeballs almost exploded in their orbits. My precious Pleyel piano had been destroyed, smashed to pieces, pummeled with a sledgehammer with the ivory keys torn asunder and the front cabriole legs twisted off and tossed in a corner of the room.

The bronze bust of Chopin no longer occupied the pseudo-Romanesque pedestal, for it was lying on the floor with Chopin's face desecrated with a hideous shade of glow-in-the-dark orange spray paint. I then went back in the living room and slowly cracked open the door to the walk-in closet where I kept my other precious instruments. The two cellos, the several violins, the Gibson guitars, and the fold-up Italian harpsichord had been reduced to a pile of splinters, unrecognizable for what they once were except for the headstock of one of the guitars emblazoned with "Gibson," and a twisted mélange of wire strings from the guitars and the harpsichord.

There was no doubt in my mind that I knew the perpetrator of this horrible crime. It was that fucking cunt bitch Dolores who despite what I had been told by the old man at the crematorium, had definitely survived the fires of the oven. In fact, I was thoroughly convinced that she had awoke from her weird slumbers before being placed in the oven, and that the old man at the crematorium was a lying son of a bitch that deserved to be roasted on a spit like a pig cut in half for a Texas barbeque. For all intents and purposes, this was the darkest hour of my miserable life, especially when I realized I had one more thing to accomplish to bring my task to a satisfactory conclusion. I had to find that cunt whore Dolores and put a fucking bullet in her brain and then pay tribute to old Albert Fish by stripping her naked and slicing some tender meaty strips from her jellied gasoline ass with a dull butter knife so I could enjoy a nice late-night dinner.

But since life is indeed a bucketful of shit with a barbed wire handle that cuts into your hand like a fucking razor blade, my fantasy about enjoying a late-night snack composed of slices of flesh from Dolores' jellied gasoline ass did not come to pass. Recall those medical pamphlets that I stole from the New York Public Library and hid in a plain brown envelope in a desk drawer? Well, when I thought about the pamphlets and how they could possibly implicate me in the death of that cunt bitch Dolores, I discovered that they were gone. But how could this be, knowing that I was the only person on this fucked-up planet that knew the pamphlets were hidden in the desk drawer? The answer is quite simple; in fact, it's so simple that I'm not even going to mention it. Let's just say that *her* hands were in that drawer at some point.

As I stood there pondering the ruins of my once-beautiful Pleyel piano, I suddenly heard soft footsteps coming from somewhere. Not a living soul knew that I had returned to New York City, so I found it rather odd that someone had decided to pay me a visit. Have you ever read Edgar Poe's *Fall of the House of Usher?* Certain descriptions in the opening paragraph of this weird Gothic tale perfectly conveys how I felt upon hearing those soft footsteps. When the footsteps became a bit louder, I felt a sharp pain

in what must've been the lower corner of my left ventricle. As Poe numb-
ingly expresses it, the unknown narrator of this tale experiences a sense
of insufferable gloom upon his first glimpse of the House of Usher and
is overcome by an utter depression of his soul which he compares to "no
earthly sensation" except for the "after-dream" that arises following the
ingestion of opium; then, the "bitter lapse into everyday life" or *knowing*
that doom is right around the corner.

Lastly, the "hideous dropping off of the veil" that conceals the reali-
ties of death, then a "sickening of the heart," much like a ghostly hand
reaching inside one's chest and grasping the beating organ until the blood
stops flowing. These sensations and several others came upon me rather
slowly at first until I found myself standing face-to-face with that cunt
bitch Dolores in all her naked putridness, standing near the remains of
my beautiful Pleyel piano, with her skin and hair burnt to a crisp and the
blueness of her eyes clashing with the anthracite blackness of her orbits.

"Hello, Carl. Nice to see you again."

By simply observing the expression on her scarred and mutilated face,
I was absolutely certain that Dolores had killed my life-long friend and
confident Pierre Lamontaigne, and that she had deliberately destroyed
my precious Pleyel piano, probably with the same sledgehammer that I
bought several years ago to break up an old sidewalk that ran from the
house to the street. I was also wholly convinced that she had been at
Chopin's tomb in Paris, whispering and moaning from the void of darkness and causing young Violette to flee from the cemetery. It was also
clear that Dolores had stirred in the ovens of the furnace as the flames
seared her jellied gasoline ass, probably in the middle of the afternoon
when everyone had gone to Flannagan's tavern across the street to drown
the stench of death in a couple flagons of MacGillicutty's Scottish ale.

And then I thought, "Well, here she is, that cunt bitch, standing less
than three feet from me. Let's put an end to all the bullshit right now."

I went to a clothes closet and opened it to reveal leaning against the
drywall in the left-hand corner old uncle Charlie's 45. caliber Thompson
sub-machine gun, the original "chopper" that he allegedly utilized to
cut to pieces those poor fucking bastards of the North Side gang on St.
Valentine's Day in 1929 at the Lincoln Park garage. As soon as I had
this formidable weapon in my hands, I drew back the bolt and pointed
it at Dolores.

"Here, ya fucking cunt bitch," I said. "Suck on this."

And with that, I pulled the trigger, releasing a spray of bullets that tore
into Dolores' body, causing huge holes to open up with blood spurting

everywhere and chucks of flesh flying against the walls and ceiling, cling-ing to the plaster like slices of yellow peaches. I can't really say how many slugs of lead ended up in her jellied ass carcass, but within a few moments, the gun clicked off, an indication that the clip was empty. Suffice it to say that Dolores was no longer standing by the Pleyel piano because what was left of her body was lying on the floor like a pile of burnt pork chops. Dolores was, for all intents and purposes, nothing more than a mass of putridness with one of her blue eyes peeking out from what was left of her face.

Early this morning after being specially served with a plateful of bacon and eggs with some sausage on the side, I was handed the following letter from Mr. Robert Fitzsimmons, the fucking warden of Sing-Sing prison who overall is a pretty nice guy, considering how fucked-up this place is and his sworn duty to carry out the executions of the people deemed by the state of New York as incorrigibles with myself being one of them. Although I've provided quite a bit of information about myself to the readers of this "manifesto," the warden must be congratulated for adding to my scant biography. However, I must warn you at this point in my digressions that everything Mr. Fitzsimmons says is a bold-faced, fucking lie from beginning to end. Not a single word of it is true or accurate. He is nothing but a mythomaniac, a "pseudologia fantasticum" and a fabulist that deserves to have his bare ass jammed in that bucketful of shit with the barbed wire handle:

Dear Mr. Underwood;

The letter that is now in your hands is mandated under the penal and institutional protocols of the State of New York in relation to your confinement at this facility. It is our deepest wish not to create additional suffering for you, but under the circumstances, this is unfortunately not possible, due to your constant refusal to live in reality. But regardless, as warden of this facility, I must relate the following to you:

The inmate, Mr. Carl Underwood, was indicted on September 18, 1967, for murder in the first degree, in that he killed his wife Dolores Underwood with a Thompson sub-machine gun at his home in Riverdale, New York. At the time of the alleged killing, Mr. Underwood was a retired member of the New York Philharmonic with a specialty in the music of Frederick Chopin. At this moment, Mr. Underwood is sixty-six years old. He and his wife were married for twenty-five years and according to the testimonies of their friends and colleagues, their marriage was singularly devoted. However, the State of New York has been unable to confirm whether Mr. Underwood actually murdered his wife Dolores. Her physical remains have not been located, nor have any witnesses to the alleged crime come forward.

Mr. Underwood has admitted to killing his wife by having her burned alive in the crematorium associated with the Bronx County Health Department and the Bronx-Lebanon Hospital, but like his admission of guilt, the State of New York has been unable to determine if Mr. Underwood's story is accurate or merely a figment of his vast imagination. As per the laws of the great State of New York, when an individual admits to a heinous crime and pleads with the acting attorney general and the court to accept his guilty plea, the State has no other alternative than to accept his admission of guilt. However, it is of our opinion and of those in other institutions, that Mr. Carl Underwood is mentally unstable; he is, in fact, quite mad.

Well, there it is. It still pisses me off to know that the warden of this fucked-up place known as Sing-Sing prison and the authorities of the State of New York just don't believe my story about killing that cunt bitch Dolores. If they don't believe me, then what the fuck am I doing here in the first place? I should be able to wander the streets of the city like Albert Fish in search of smooth and fleshy buttocks ripe for the frying pan and tiny penises that I can keep in aqua Ball Mason jars on a shelf next to a mantel clock. Speaking of clocks…

Take a look at the pasty concrete wall behind me. See that round Ingraham clock hanging there? The minute hand points at eight and the hour hand, heavy with black paint, edges toward twelve like a creeping ebony snake. It is now eleven-forty P.M. Take a quick glance through the iron bars set in the pasty concrete, being a small paneless window next to the clock, and you'll see nothing but blackness with the moon trying to slice out a portion of some passing clouds. In less than twenty minutes, I'll finally have my own jellied gasoline ass in the seat of "Old Sparky," waiting patiently for 2,000 volts of electricity to be hot-wired through my fucked-up brain. When they finally throw the switch, all of my suffering will be over. I wonder if I'll see old Maxie Sullivan again, or maybe Mrs. Greenburg so I can slap the shit out of her and tell her thanks for fucking up my life by introducing me to that slut whore Dolores. Maybe I'll see Pierre Lamontaigne and share a bowl of orange sherbet ice cream with him. But maybe, just maybe, I'll see Frederic Chopin in his velvet waistcoat, black jacket, and pair of gray trousers that look like they've been recently ironed. They say that time is irrelevant when you're dead, so hopefully I'll see that fucking old man that talks like Burt Lancaster someday so I can smash him in the face with a shovel.

A Final Prelude

At around eight o'clock this morning, I woke up from a deep and somber sleep, and as soon as my eyelids fluttered open, I knew that I was Frederic Chopin, for here I was, lying in a soft, down-filled bed with ruffled white blankets covering my feet and legs and the rest of my torso wrapped in a clean white straightjacket with nice shiny chrome buckles. At the foot of my bed stood George Sand with an exceptional grimace on her ugly face, the kind that one might see on the face of a visitor who knows that the occupant of a particular hospital bed is near death. But alas! No piano. Not even a picture of one. How is it possible for Chopin to experience any sort of pleasure or contentment without a piano in his midst? On my left side, Dr. John Moran, the attending physician here at the institution, squatted in a chair while writing something on a thick pad of paper clipped to a board. When I smiled at him, he knew that I wanted to know what he was writing. He also knew that it was nothing but sheer compulsion that was responsible for my present situation, strapped to a bed for the remainder of my natural life.

"All right, Carl," he said. "Remember that book I mentioned to you several months ago, the one I was thinking about writing? Well, this is part of the introduction:

"It pains me to no extent to relate that Mr. Carl Underwood is one of the saddest lost souls I have ever known as a professional medical man. I say this because in fact, Mr. Carl Underwood is insane, and as his physician, I can attest to the fact that his tendencies toward insanity are due to what I refer to as predisposing factors or causes which have brought about his particular madness. I have known many men who through inheritance have been prone to insanity despite being highly educated and specializing in a specific area of pursuit, such as music or painting.

In Carl's case, pathological manifestations have been acquired from the outside world that have left permanent mental scars in his mind. In essence, Carl's insanity is the result of overstrain and enormous fatigue, both of which have created a poisonous effect on his mind. In effect, Carl exhibits what are commonly known as idiopathic tendencies, due to the loss of moral causes that have left him unable to distinguish between reality and fantasy.

The main factor here is the existence of a long-continued strain in relation to his wife Dolores who, to the best of my professional knowledge, still resides in her home in Riverdale. This long-continued strain is due to Carl's obsession with murdering Dolores which has severely damaged the nerve cells in his brain and its associated cerebral circulations. In essence, Carl's mind has become clogged (for the lack of a better word) with the products of wasteful and time-consuming thoughts. It is my belief that Carl somehow believes that Dolores is George Sand, thus creating the idea that she must die for possibly contributing to Chopin's early death.

In addition, I would like to briefly discuss another aspect related to Carl's mental health that I feel is absolutely necessary to understand his condition at this time. It is my professional opinion that Carl Underwood suffers from what is known as temporal lobe epilepsy which would explain many of his wild hallucinations and what I call his "madness visions of death." By the strangest of coincidences, some musical researchers have long suspected that Frederic Chopin suffered from the same exact affliction. For example, in 1848 while performing at a private residence in Paris, Chopin suddenly stopped playing, stood up, and walked away, leaving his audience in a state of utter confusion.

Later on, Chopin wrote to an anonymous friend and admitted that he saw some strange creatures emerge from inside his half-open piano case. Chopin also reportedly saw weird phantoms and demons lurking about in his house. However, Chopin never mentions anything about hearing strange sounds or noises, a distinctive reference for hallucinations generated by temporal lobe epilepsy. But in Carl's case, the hallucinatory sounds that he so often described could be generated by something entirely different, thus making it possible that his auditory system has also been destroyed.

To be blunt, everything that Mr. Underwood has discussed and revealed in his "manifesto" is a complete and utter lie, an extremely complex and dense fantasy which he believes is true and factual. His wife Dolores is alive and healthy and does not suffer from any sort of preconceived illnesses, especially catalepsy. His precious Pleyel piano, as well as his other antique instruments, are still safe and sound under the guardianship of his wife and a few of Carl's friends from his days at the New York Philharmonic. Mr. Pierre Lamontaigne is a fictional abstract, and Mr. Underwood has never visited the beautiful city of Paris nor has he spent any amount of time in Chopin's "haunted house," known locally as the Chateau d'Herouville.

In addition, I have heard Carl say some very odd things in his sleep while under sedation, such as begging for the forgiveness of a woman named Sybil Vane, and saying that he is sorry for tossing another woman named Wanda Jackson out of an apartment building window five stories above the street. On one occasion, Carl mentioned someone called Violette whom he addresses as his French sweetheart. But the most shocking revelation came when Carl was under the influence of a powerful hypnotic drug. To the best of my recollection, he said something like this:

"I think it was on Halloween eve when the idea of murdering my wife first came to me.

Exactly why I wanted her dead is difficult to explain, but one thing was certain. For the longest time, I found myself haunted by a myriad of disturbing fantasies that should only occur in a nightmare, such as how it would feel to see Dolores lying in a freshly-dug grave while wearing nothing but the skin she was born in or how delightful it would be to cut a peephole in the side of her casket and watch her fucked-up body being eaten by worms and maggots."

"Well, Carl," asked Dr. Moran. "What do you think?"

"I think you're a fucking son of a bitch that should be roasted to death, or better yet, deep-fried in a skillet with some pureed dick sauce."

"OK, Carl. Just settle down. Maybe this'll help."

The padded door to Carl's cell swings open to reveal two male attendants in white uniforms pushing a chrome hospital gurney holding a stereo amplifier and a turntable. After rolling the gurney into the cell, one of the attendants leaves for a moment, then returns carrying two small speakers. He wires the speakers to the amp, turns it on.

"What would you like to hear, Carl?" asks Dr. Moran, while writing in his notebook.

"You know what I wanna fucking hear. Why do you torture me like this?"

"I'm not torturing you, Carl. I'm a doctor, not a Grand Inquisitor."

"Yes, you are! You're nothing but a fucking son of a bitch, just like the rest of those bastards around here."

"Are you referring to the doctors here at the hospital?"

"Of course. They're a bunch of fucking cocksuckers. Have you seen that cunt bitch Dolores around here? If I could only get my hands on her, I'd…"

"What would you do, Carl?"

"I'd stick my hand up her cunt and pull out her guts."

"That would be quite messy."

Doctor Moran slides a waxen LP from a worn cardboard jacket with Eugene Delacroix's image of Frederic Chopin dominating the water-stained cover. Big blue letters proclaim THE PRELUDES OF FREDERIC CHOPIN.

"Is this what you want to hear?"

"Of course, ya fucking idiot. Better than that fucking Wanda Jackson!"

"Sorry. Don't know the lady."

Moran puts the LP on the turntable, lowers the tonearm. Moments later, Carl's cell is filled with the rhapsodic delicacy of Chopin's beautiful piano music. Carl becomes unusually reticent. His lips move indistinctly for a few moments, then recoil into a satisfied smile reminiscent of sweet Violette at Chopin's tomb in Pere Lachaise Cemetery. As Moran retrieves his chair and starts writing again in his notepad, jotting down random thoughts and figments of his own psychiatric imagination, a figure fills the open portal to Carl's cell, casting a pitch-black shadow across the pure whiteness of Carl's clean straightjacket.

"Who's that at my chamber door?" asks Carl. "'Tis a very late visitor, I assume. Maybe it's that Polish Catholic clergyman from my funeral."

The shade draws closer to Carl's bed. As it stands at the foot of the bed, two arms like the necks of dead swans emerge from a cloak lined with crimson. The arms reach upward and draw back a black hood, revealing the face of Dolores Underwood, beautiful to behold and beautiful long before Carl knew of her existence. In fact, Dolores is so strikingly beautiful that Carl fails to recognize her. Her hair is long and auburn; her eyes glow with the intensity of two pale blue candle flames; her lips are swollen like the petals of a cunt; and her skin is ghastly white, as white as the underbelly of Cygnus, the beautiful prowler of the River Seine that flows through the city of Paris. And then, like a burning streak of napalm among the Flame trees of Vietnam, fire red against a vivid blue sky, Carl realizes the identity of the shade at the foot of his bed.

"Fuck you, Dolores!" he screams. "I hope you burn in Hell, ya fucking cunt bitch!"

And of course, since it is always superior to reign in Hell than serve in Heaven under the watchful eyes of a jealous and evil God, Dolores Underwood can at last smile with contentive vengeance, knowing that Carl, her insane husband, will be thoroughly dead when the last bass note sounds on Chopin's Prelude in D minor, Op. 28, No. 24, the simple "prelude" of Dorian Gray and Miss Sibyl Vane with the little stuffed yellow bird nesting in her straw hat. And as the final bass note tumbles from the speakers, Carl Underwood, a pathological liar with madness in his heart and an undying love for the music of Frederic Chopin, closes his eyes and grins despite the invisible pain that radiates like fire when one's heart is ripped out while still alive and placed in a jar filled with French brandy. George Sand(ers) understands it perfectly. It is a Prelude to Death in D minor, a gust of piano music wafting from a garden filled with roses, nightingales, and violets being gently caressed by the fingers of a slut.

About The Author

Originally from Paris, France, MICHEL MARCHAUD is the author of a number of books that have never been finished and probably never will be. Like most writers, he is the proud possessor of a drawerful of manuscripts that should be tossed in the nearest roaring fireplace. He served with distinction in that fucked-up conflict known as Vietnam in 1973 and admits that he is probably responsible for the deaths of thousands of Vietnamese. Like most of his naval comrades, Marchaud became a roaring alcoholic and stayed drunk for forty-two years until his heart gave out in 2014. He is now sober but does not enjoy it.

Public Domain Sources

Baudelaire, Charles. *My Heart Laid Bare and Other Prose Writings.* Trans. Norman Cameron. London: 1950. [Originally published Paris, 1897].

Blake, George W. *Report on Sing-Sing Prison.* State of New York: Albany, 1913.

Blandford, G. Fielding. *Insanity.* New York: William Wood, 1897.

Chapin, Charles. *Charles Chapin's Story, Written in Sing-Sing Prison.* New York and London: Knickerbocher Press, 1920.

Coleridge, Samuel Taylor. *Marriage.* London: Printed for Private Circulation, 1919.

Cortot, Alfred. *Frederic Chopin, 24 Preludes.* Paris: 1930.

Dutton, Ralph, and Lord Holden. *The Land of France.* London: B.T. Batsford, Ltd., 1939.

Ferra, Bartomeu. *Chopin and George Sand in Majorca.* Spain: Palma de Mallorca, 1936.

Fraser, John, & C.F. Folsom. "A Scotch Insane Asylum." Fife and Kinross District Lunatic Asylum. Rpt. "The Boston Medical and Surgical Journal," August 12, 1875. 1-12.

Groves, Sir George. *A Dictionary of Music and Musicians, 1450-1889.* Vol. III. London: MacMillan & Co., 1889.

Hadden, J. Cuthbert. *Chopin.* London: J.M. Dent & Co., New York: E.P. Dutton & Co., 1903.

Liszt, Franz. *Life of Chopin.* London: William Reeves, Ltd., 1877.

Ramul, Peter. The Psycho-Physical Foundations of Modern Piano Technique. *Leipzig, Germany: C.F. Kahnt, 1931.*

Sand, George. "Un hiver a Majorque" (A Winter in Majorca). Paris: Revue des deux Mondes, 1841.

_____. *Histoire de ma vie.* [The Story of My Life]. Paris: Victor Lecou, ed., 1854.

Solly, Thomas. *The Will: Divine and Human.* London: Bell and Daldy, 1856.

Stekel, Wilhelm. *Sadism and Masochism: The Psychology of Hatred and Cruelty.* Vol. 1. New York: Liveright Publishing Corporation, 1939.

Tapper, Thomas, and Percy Goetschius. *Essentials in Music History.* New York: Charles Scribner's Sons, 1923.

Non Public Domain Sources

Cortot, Alfred. *In Search of Chopin.* London: Peter Nevill, Ltd., 1951.

Karasowski, Moritz. *Frederic Chopin: His Life and Letters.* 3rd. ed. London: William Reeves, Ltd., 1938.

Kildea, Paul. Chopin's Piano: In Search of the Instrument that Transformed Music. *New York: W.W. Norton & Company, 2018.*

Kirkconnell, Watson. "The Genius of Slavic Poetry." *Dalhousie Review,* Vol. 9 issue no. 4, 1930: 500-506.

Kirkpatrick, Ralph. *Cortot: Early Years.* New York: Peter Lang, 1985.

Landowska, Wanda. *Wanda Landowska and Denise Restout papers.* 1894. Manuscript/Mixed Material. Library of Congress. *https://lccn.loc.gov/2013568041.*

Sydow, B.E., ed. *Selected Correspondence of Fryderyk Chopin.* UK: William Heinemann Ltd., 1962.

Wheeler, Opal. *Frederic Chopin, Son of Poland: The Early Years.* New York: E.P. Dutton & Co., 1949.